DANCING THROUGH LIFE
BOOK NINE

MAN
OF THE
Month

PATRICIA M. ROBERTSON

"The course of true love never did run smooth." *(Shakespeare)*

Sometimes you have to kiss a lot of frogs before you find your prince. Take a chance on love anyway!

"As soon as I saw you, I knew an adventure was about to happen." (Winnie the Pooh)

Chapter 1

Laura sipped her wine and observed the three women as they chattered and nibbled on cheese and crackers. They didn't know it, but they were about to embark on an adventure of her making.

"I suppose you are wondering why I asked you here," she began.

"I heard there would be cake," Margie stated as she popped a piece of cheese in her mouth.

"There will be, but first, to the business at hand." Laura moved forward in her seat, perching on the chair and preparing to pounce. "You are my oldest and dearest friends."

"We first met three years ago in the support group," Hattie said.

"Okay, so you are my newest and dearest friends."

"Sounds about right," Hattie stated.

It was a mistake, inviting the women from her depression support group to be part of this mission. Too honest. Her mission required some ability to lie and deceive. But she had burned through many friendships back when in the throes of depression. All those years, gone, lost in a murky haze of gloom. All those years when she had relied on Gwen. Now it was time for Gwen to rely on her; time to pay Gwen back for all of her sacrifice. If she could just get Gwen to see it that way.

Through the grace of God, new meds, a new way of thinking and acting, and her support group, she had found her way back. Whenever she found herself slipping back into old ways of thinking and behaving, they challenged her, helped her keep from that sinkhole that had been her life. They appreciated her flippant sense of humor, loved her despite it. They challenged her when she needed it, supported her even when not worthy of support. Even though she had only known them for the past three years, she felt they knew her better than anyone else in her life, including her husband. He would not have any part in this. That's why she needed them, her friends. They had helped her dig out of the dark hole that had been her life. Who else could she trust?

"You all know my daughter, Gwen."

"Of course, a lovely girl. How is she doing in seminary?" Hattie asked. Laura had often talked of Gwen during their meetings.

"She's coming here to St. Luke's for her internship."

"That's wonderful. What great news," was heard from all sides.

"What do you need from us?" Hattie asked.

"I need your help getting her to stay in Cascade Falls."

"Now, Laura," Hattie shook her head. "You know that's up to her."

"Yeah, the last thing I wanted at her age was to stay in my home town. Anything my mom would have tried to keep me there would have just pushed me further away," Bernice added.

"That's why she can't know I'm behind this."

"Behind what? What are you up to now?" Bernice asked.

Laura pulled out a poster board. In the middle was a picture of her daughter. Around her, like hands on a clock, were the months of the year with a man's picture taped below each. Across the top in large letters was written, Man of the Month Club.

"What's this?" Hattie asked.

"The Man of the Month Club. Don't you get it?" Laura presented the poster with a wave of her hand. "Our goal is to find a new eligible bachelor for Gwen to date every month until she finds Mr. Right. Like Bachelorette, but over a longer period of time and without all the money."

"It will never work," Hattie stated.

"Hey, who wouldn't want to go out with my daughter? Just look at that face. How could any man resist?"

"Gwen will never go along with this. You'll just push her away. It's a recipe for disaster," Bernice said.

"She never needs to know. We set up everything. We find ways for them to bump into each other. You know, like on the elevator at work or they bump into each other going out a door and dump a bunch of papers on the ground. They reach down at the same time to pick up the same piece of paper. Their fingers touch. They look into each other's eyes. It's kismet. You've seen those Hallmark movies, haven't you?"

"Yes, and it doesn't work like that in real life," Hattie stated.

"And she's working for the church. The church doesn't have an elevator," Bernice added. "Might as well give up before we begin. It'll never work."

"Who says it can't happen like that? Anyway, we give the man of the month Gwen's phone number and pertinent details about her. He has one month to win her over. If not successful after one month, we move on to the next prey, er, man."

"Gwen's a smart girl. She'll figure it out," Hattie said.

"Gwen may be smart, but not where men are concerned. That's why she needs a little help from us."

"I don't know." Hattie shook her head.

"She'll thank us for it. You know how hard it is for a single woman to find a man once they're out of college?"

"Try finding a man once you turn thirty. My daughter will never get married and give me grandkids," Bernice stated.

"What do we have to do?" Margie asked.

"Each of you have to find three eligible men, mid-to-late twenties, early thirties. What do you say? Are you in? There'll be cake." Laura poured more wine into their glasses.

"What's in it for us?" Hattie asked.

"My undying gratitude?" The expressions on her friends' faces told her that was clearly not enough. "Okay, a hundred dollars to the one who finds Mr. Right."

"Not nearly enough," Hattie stated.

"Five hundred?"

"Better." Hattie shook her head, negotiating for all three.

"My tennis bracelet?" Laura held her hand out for all to examine the bracelet.

"Getting closer," Hattie said.

Laura pulled back her hand. "The Thunderbird? You can't expect my convertible? I love that car." The smiles on all three faces told her she was wrong.

"But you love your daughter more," Hattie stated.

"That I do," Laura agreed. "Okay. The one who provides the boyfriend who will put a ring on my daughter's finger will get the … the Thunderbird." The word caught in her throat as she said it, coming out like a stutter.

"I'm in. When do we start?" Hattie said.

"You had me at cake," Margie replied.

"I'll assign each of you three months. That means you have to come up with three eligible bachelors."

"Three times three," Margie said. "That's only nine months."

"Because I'm part of this too. I'm not giving up my Thunderbird that easily. What about you, Bernice?"

"I still say it won't work. It's bound to end up in a disaster or worse, but, if the rest of you are in," Bernice shrugged. "I am too. Besides, that Thunderbird would look awfully good sitting in my driveway, though that will never happen."

"When do we start?" Hattie asked.

"As soon as we find bachelor number one," Laura stated as they clicked their wine glasses. "To Gwen! We'll be the four musketeers. All for one, and one for all."

"Here's to the Thunderbird," Hattie stated and raised her glass. "Every woman for herself."

"I'll drink to that as well," Laura said. "Let the game begin."

Chapter 2

Back to Cascade Falls. It's like she's stuck in a bad movie. Or that movie, "Groundhog Day," where the hero can't get out of Punxutawney and is doomed to repeat the same day over and over again. Or her dad's favorite movie, "It's a Wonderful Life," where every time George Bailey is on the brink of leaving Bedford Falls, some crisis keeps him there.

But how could Gwen not come home after her dad's heart attack?

"Your brothers and sister didn't have any problem staying away so they didn't have to help out," her friend Marcie reminded her.

"They have family concerns."

"And excuses. All three of them. Why do you always have to be the one who takes care of your mom and dad?"

"It will just be for a year. Then I'll be ordained and sent somewhere else. You never stay in the church you do your internship in. I'll be associate pastor at some church far away from Cascade Falls."

"Just be careful," Marcie had warned her. She didn't need the warning. Gwen knew far too well that her mother was intent on having her move home, live out her days the way she had lived her life for the first twenty years, in Cascade Falls, answering to her mother's whims.

"I don't see why you have to move into that musty old place when you have a perfectly beautiful room at home," her mother had insisted when she gave Gwen the key to the manse.

"Because living in the house the church provides is part of the intern experience," Gwen had asserted. It wasn't a requirement, but her mother didn't need to know that. "I need to understand what life in a manse is like before deciding whether to go forward with ordination."

"How can you help your dad, living so far away?"

"Mom, it's a short drive, and dad is doing great. I can be there in five minutes if you need me."

"It's not the same."

"That's right. I need new experiences. I need to be available to church members too."

Gwen picked up the key and slid out the door. "I can show myself in," she said as she left her mother at the desk that once was her desk, back when she had served her term as church secretary. Her mother had been hired for the position after she left for seminary. As far as she knew, her mother was doing fine in the role.

Gwen had been relieved to move to Chicago back then. Chicago had everything she wanted. Night life, excitement, many different cultures. Besides her seminary classes, she had minored in Chicago. She couldn't wait to go back. What was a year to help out her dad?

She turned the key, opened the door and was hit with a blast of musty hot air. How long had the place been shut up? She didn't remember it being that bad when Pastor Joe had lived there. How long had it been since the previous intern had moved out? One month? Two? She pulled her suitcase through the door and proceeded to open windows.

"Settling in?" A familiar voice sounded in the hallway.

"Marcie?" Gwen embraced her friend. "What are you doing here? How did you get in?"

"The door was unlocked. You didn't think I'd let my best friend make the biggest mistake of her life without me? I'm here to rescue you, at least for tonight."

"Who needs rescuing?" Another familiar voice. Pastor Joe. Her boss.

"No one," Gwen assured him, giving Marcie a cautionary look.

"I came to welcome you and see if you would like to have dinner with us tonight. You're welcome too, Marcie."

"Is your wife cooking?" Gwen asked.

"She's gotten better," Pastor Joe assured her, "But no, Kathleen won't be cooking. I'm grilling burgers."

"That's okay, Pastor, but you have all year with Gwen. I'm taking her out tonight, right Gwen?"

"What she said." Gwen nodded in Marcie's direction.

"Another time then. Let me know if you need anything," Pastor Joe said as Marcie escorted him out.

"Now, let's get you settled, then I'm taking you to the Crab Shack," Marcie told her.

"You're not coming home for dinner?" Yet another familiar voice. Her mother took Pastor Joe's spot in the room. She would have to start locking that front door.

"Sorry, Mom. What Marcie said."

"Not tonight, Mrs. Thompson. Tonight, it's just us girls."

"Then breakfast tomorrow. Both of you," her mother insisted.

Gwen looked at Marcie before answering. "Sure, Mom. Just not too early."

"Brunch then. Eleven o'clock. It's all settled."

Again Marcie opened the front door, escorting Gwen's mother out. She locked the door this time. "Now, no more interruptions."

"That was surprisingly easy," Gwen commented. Her mom didn't usually give up so quickly.

"Nothing to worry about. Let's get you settled so we can get out of this place."

Gwen went along with Marcie. Her mom was up to something but nothing that couldn't wait until tomorrow to be dealt with.

Chapter 3

The Crab Shack was crowded despite being the middle of the week. On Wednesdays during the summer months they had a band playing on the patio for all of the summer residents.

They found a table inside and ordered a pizza.

"Marcie, Gwen, it's good to see you," the waitress said. They both looked at her but couldn't put a name to the face.

"I'm Debbie, don't you remember me?" she asked. "From sixth hour American history."

"Oh, that Debbie," Marcie said. "Good to see you. How are you doing?"

"As well as I can," Debbie said, then took their orders.

"Maybe this was a mistake," Marcie said as another waitress came up and said hi. "All these people from high school. I wasn't looking for a reunion tonight."

"Me either, but I guess I better get used to it. I'll be running into a lot of people I know. That's the problem with doing my internship in my home town. All these people who think they know you, who remember you from high school. It can be hard to break out of the expectations that come with those memories. Pastor Joe and I had talked about it before I accepted the position."

"Yet you still decided to come back."

"It can be a challenge or it can be an asset. It all depends on how you look at it."

"No matter how I look at it, it's still Cascade Falls. Is it too late to get out of this internship?"

"Yes. Besides, I don't want to get out of it. There's still my dad to consider."

"How's he doing?"

"Much better. He told me he doesn't need any help. He's making changes to his diet, beginning an exercise routine. He's even going back to work part-time."

"See, there's no reason for you to stay here."

"Yeah, but there's my mom. She needs help taking care of my dad." Gwen paused to take a piece of the pizza Debbie placed on their table, pulling off long threads of cheese.

"She seemed fine to me." Marcie grabbed a piece as well. Marcie was all too aware of Gwen's mom's history with depression. Gwen had been her mother's caretaker throughout high school, missing out on many significant events because of her mom.

"She does. 'Seems' is the operative word. I can't trust it, not with my dad's health problems. I can't risk her having a setback."

"So once again you sacrifice your life for your mom's. You may end up here for the rest of your life. There will always be another crisis where your mom is concerned."

"No, just this one year. You know, she has a group of friends. I think they are from her support group. And that Thunderbird convertible of hers. Who'd have thought all it would take is a classic car to get mom out of her depressive state."

"I'm sure it took more than that."

"She loves that car. She drives all over town with the top down during the summer. Her and those friends of hers. I think she's reliving her youth."

Marcie shrugged and reached for another piece of pizza. "If it keeps her happy and out of your way, what's wrong with it?"

"Enough of this. Let's finish off this pizza then go dance." Gwen grabbed the last piece and washed it down with a beer.

They ordered a bucket of beer to take outside to the crowded patio. A man Gwen vaguely remembered from high school approached them.

"Marcie Taylor? Is that you?"

"Last I checked."

"Last I heard you were studying to be a reporter somewhere in Chicago."

"You heard correctly. Brad, right?"

"What brings you back?"

"My friend here. You remember Gwen." Marcie pulled Gwen forward.

"Sure … Gwen – Dr. Thompson's daughter, right?" Brad barely glanced at Gwen before turning back to Marcie. "You look amazing, Marcie."

"Gwen is going to be doing her internship at St. Luke's."

"That's great. You want to join us?" Brad pointed to a table with two men, also vaguely familiar. Gwen squirmed and whispered no in Marcie's ear.

"Sure, why not?" Marcie said and followed Brad to his table. Gwen pulled on her arm to stop her.

"Hey, look," Marcie said, "there are no free tables, no seats anywhere that I can see. This will give us a place to put our beer and sit. It will be fine. You said you need to get used to running into people you know."

They were at the table before Gwen had a chance to respond. They sat their bucket down and sat in the seats newly vacated for them. Brad pulled up a chair next to Marcie and talked non-stop. The two other men stood by the table, beer bottles in hand, ignoring Gwen. It was just like back in high school again. Marcie had been Miss Popularity. Gwen had been too busy taking care of her mom to make many friends beyond Marcie. That had changed in college, but here she was, back in high school, ignored while the boys hang on Marcie's words. Could it get any worse?

"You're Gwen, aren't you? Dr. Thompson's daughter?"

It just got worse. A man in glasses and a short-sleeved button-down shirt, buttoned to the top, approached her.

"Leon, remember me? We were lab partners."

"Leon, sure, I remember." She remembered him almost blowing up the lab with his "rocket fuel" or whatever it was he had invented.

What chance of fate had assigned him as her lab partner? Mr. Stuckey had it out for her. She had been sure of that. Now here he was. Another memory from high school she would rather forget.

"I hear you're the new intern at St. Luke's."

"That's right. What do you do?"

"I work at Sears in the Automotive Department. I'm an engine specialist. I run diagnostics on car engines."

"They allow you around all of that flammable substances even after your escapades in chem lab?"

"Because of them. You want to dance?"

Gwen looked at Marcie for assistance. Marcie was deep in conversation with Brad. No help there. She might as well make the best of things. Gwen stood up, her five foot ten inches towering over Leon's five foot five.

"You haven't grown much since high school," she commented.

"My mom says I'm a late bloomer. She's still waiting for that last growth spurt."

"Right." Gwen finished off her beer and started for the dance floor.

"You sure you should be doing that?" Leon asked.

"Doing what?"

"Drinking. You are studying to be a minister, aren't you? Not that I mind, but others ..."

Gwen looked back at Marcie. Marcie smiled and waved at her. As soon as the song ended, Gwen thanked Leon then went back to the table.

"Ladies room, now!" she grabbed Marcie and yelled in her ear.

"What's wrong?" Marcie asked once they reached the confines of the restroom.

"Didn't you see me?"

"Yes, you looked like you were having fun."

"With Leon? Never mind. Let's get out of here."

"In case you didn't notice, I've been talking you up to Brad."

"That what you call it?"

"Sure. I'm going back to Chicago. You're the one staying here. I'm getting you some dates so you won't be sitting alone in that manse once I'm gone. See, I've got Brad's number and his two friends as well." Marcie showed her the numbers on a napkin.

"In case you haven't noticed, they aren't interested."

"They just don't know you yet."

"Are you my mom or what?"

"Just a friend trying to help a friend."

"Maybe I don't need that kind of help."

"Okay. I'm sorry. We came here to dance. Let's go out there and dance." When they came back to their table, all of the beer in the bucket was gone, drunk by Brad and his friends.

"Come on, doll. Let's you and me dance." Brad stepped up to Marcie. When she resisted, he clasped her hand tightly and started to pull her out on the dance floor.

"Stop it, Brad." Marcie tried to pull away. Leon stepped forward.

"You heard her. She doesn't want to dance with you."

"Let her go," Gwen intervened.

"Yeah, let her go," Leon added.

"Or what?" Brad responded.

"Or this." Gwen grabbed the bucket of icy water and dumped it on Brad before he had a chance to punch Leon.

"There a problem here?" A tall lean man stepped between Brad and Gwen and flashed a badge.

"No, officer," Brad responded.

"That's good because I'm off duty. Wouldn't be happy about having to take you in on my night off."

"No, sir. No problem."

"Then I suggest you go get cleaned up and leave the ladies alone."

Brad and his buddies scurried away.

"You two okay?" the officer asked Gwen and Marcie. Gwen noted a ripple of muscle under his t-shirt. His deep blue eyes, square jaw and short light brown hair were the perfect complement to her hair and delicate features, she found herself thinking.

"Miss?" the officer said when she didn't respond.

"We're fine," Marcie answered for both of them.

"Aren't you the two young women who helped us crack that trafficking case at the nail salon?"

"Guilty," Gwen said. "Our one claim to fame."

"And didn't I take you to the hospital that night —"

"Right again." Gwen didn't let him finish. She didn't want to be reminded about that Christmas Eve four years ago.

"Oh, sorry, didn't mean to bring it up. How is your mom?"

"Good, she's good," Gwen stated. He was one hunk of a man and he already knew her worst secret.

Leon stepped up. "They're fine. I'll take care of them."

"You do that." The officer smiled at him. "Well, I have to get back to my date." He nodded his head in the direction of a young woman with long, straight, blond hair. A woman befitting his hunkiness. Gwen sighed.

"Wait," Marcie stopped him. "What's your name?"

"Kelley. Liam Kelley," he stated, then gave her his card.

"Thank you, Kelley – Liam Kelley," Marcie said.

He smiled over at Gwen then left.

"He is so in to you," Marcie said once Liam was gone. She gave Gwen his card.

"In case you didn't notice, he has a girlfriend."

"Yes, but you're the girl who broke up a trafficking ring."

"I'm also the one with the crazy mother."

"Who doesn't have a crazy mother? It's just a matter of degree."

"Hey, I'm here," Leon interrupted. "In case you didn't notice, I stood up to that brute, Brad."

"Thank you, Leon. We noticed," Gwen said.

"So, will you go out with me? I have a card too." Leon handed Gwen his card.

"Okay, Leon. I'll call you," Gwen told him.

"Do you want to get more beer?" Marcie asked after Leon left.

"Nah, one basket is my limit. Why don't we go back to my 'home?' Wow, can't believe I called the manse 'home.'"

"It will be for the next year."

"We can open up a bottle of wine and watch a movie."

"Excuse me." Another interruption. Who now?

"Yes," Marcie answered.

"No, your friend. Aren't you Gwen Thompson?" The man turned to Gwen.

"Yes, and you're?"

"Gordon. My aunt is a friend of your mother's. I think we met at some family gathering." Gwen ran through faces of men she had met at some of the events her parents had dragged her to over the years. No, his face wasn't familiar, but it wasn't a bad face. Young, smooth complexion, short blond hair, just a hint of a beard, about her height. No, she would have remembered him.

"You don't remember me? We were just kids."

"Oh, that Gordon. No, I don't remember you."

"I remember you. I'm in town visiting family. Maybe we could go out sometime? Relive old memories, make new ones?"

"Maybe," Gwen answered.

"I'll call you," he said as he prepared to leave.

"You do that. Wait, you don't have my number."

"That's okay. I got it. My aunt, you know. She gave it to me."

"Your aunt. Yes," Gwen said as he left.

"Wow. You're on fire tonight. A hunky police officer and an attractive millennial."

"And don't forget Leon."

"No, who could forget Leon." They laughed as they walked out through the crowd.

"Time for that bottle of wine and movie," Gwen smiled and patted the two cards in her pocket.

Chapter 4

Gwen met with Pastor Joe the next afternoon to go over her responsibilities. Brunch with her parents had gone surprisingly well. Marcie was going to stay till Friday. Then she would be on her own.

"I'll be introducing you to the congregation this Sunday." Pastor Joe handed her a position description. "You'll be working with the youth group and young adults." Gwen expected that. Interns were usually given that assignment. It was a rite of passage for ministers. Smaller congregations couldn't afford a youth minister and those that did paid so little that the youth minister moved on to greener pastures after a year or two. "I'll also be assigning you a number of homebound church members to visit." That also was expected. The idea was to get a taste of all aspects of ministry. "We'll work out a preaching schedule next week. You'll preach once a month. You'll also attend church meetings. And the intern committee."

"Intern committee?"

"Yes, a group of church members to help you as the intern, advise you, support you." When Gwen didn't say anything, Pastor Joe added, "Was there anything else you want to do?"

"Well, Pastor, I'd like to bring the church into the 21st. century. Use more social media, podcasts, maybe incorporate drama into the service. Liven things up a bit."

"Are you saying I'm outdated?"

"No, just not up-to-date."

"We do put the weekly sermons on our website as podcasts."

"Not enough. And about those sermons …"

"Go on." Pastor Joe indicated that he was open to hearing what she had to say so she plunged forward.

"I've learned a lot of techniques through seminary and my improv classes to keep church members interested."

"You're saying I'm boring?"

"No, just your sermons don't appeal to young adults. You do want me to work with young adults, right?"

"That's part of your job description."

"Then let me help them through helping you."

"How about you start by doing what you've been assigned to do? You can work on me later. You might find it's a hopeless cause, just ask my wife."

"Your sermons show potential, Pastor. We all can use a little help now and then. No one is perfect."

"Least of all me. Anything else?"

"I'd like to start a vlog."

"A blog, like Marcie had done?" Marcie had gained some notoriety for her blog, Delicious Secrets, when she had served as secretary.

"No, a vlog. A video log. I'm not a writer like Marcie, but I would like to use my acting ability to serve God. It could be the centerpiece of my young adult ministry. I'll do a little improv, role play."

"Speaking of 'role' play. I hear you had quite the night last night, you and Marcie."

Gwen gulped. "Do you want to hear my side of the story?"

"Do I?"

"Maybe not."

"Isn't it enough that you were drinking, but to pour a bucket of ice water over a church member's head."

"He was trying to force Marcie to come with him when she didn't want to."

"I believe that Marcie can handle herself."

"Can she? Like when she was kidnapped?"

"That was different." Marcie had been taken by gun point by her grandfather five years earlier.

"I'm sorry, Pastor. It was a gut reaction. It won't happen again."

"Gwen, you're here to learn about being a pastor. Part of that is learning the role of the pastor."

"What do you mean?"

"Church members expect certain behavior from their pastors. Not engaging in drunken brawls is one of them." Gwen started to interrupt. Pastor Joe stopped her with a raise of his hand. "I know, it wasn't a drunken brawl, but it could be perceived as one. You have to be careful about your reputation. I'm not saying you can't go out with friends or have a drink, just think about appearances next time."

"But Pastor, don't you think people want a minister they can relate to? Someone human, with faults like everyone else?"

"Those faults will be far too evident as you stay in ministry. No need to add to them. Church members look to their ministers to help them be better, rise above those faults."

"Don't worry, Pastor. There won't be a next time."

"I hope not." Pastor Joe stood up to indicate their time together was over, then added. "Oh, do you have a chauffer's license?"

"No."

"You'll need one to take the youth group to the beach next weekend. You'll be driving the church van." With that she was dismissed.

The church van? Not exactly in her job description. What other surprises would the good pastor have for her?

Chapter 5

"What are we doing tonight?" Marcie asked as soon as Gwen returned. "Crab Shack again?"

"Not after last night. Someone told Pastor Joe what happened."

"I hope they also told him Brad was being a jerk."

"Brad's allowed to be a jerk. Not the intern though."

"You only stood up for me." Gwen stopped Marcie with the look, the one that said, come on, get real. "Okay. It looked bad. So we don't go to the Crab Shack. I guess other bars are out of the question as well. What else is there to do in this town?"

"You know as well as I do."

"Karaoke?"

"Another bar."

"Okay. I guess it's burgers, then a movie in the safe confines of the manse."

"That is probably the best option."

They went to their favorite burger joint and were surprised when a man sauntered over to their booth and leaned on the table.

"I hear you're the new intern at St. Luke's."

"Yes," Gwen responded. "And you are?"

"Just someone who might start going to church, if you know what I mean."

"No, I don't know what you mean."

"Aren't you here to save souls? I'm a lost soul, looking for someone to save me." He winked, and nodded his head, his smile showing a set of dazzling pearly white teeth. His dark hair was puffed up into a pompadour. Marcie rolled her eyes back into her head.

"Really?" Gwen responded, trying to avoid the look on Marcie's face lest she break out laughing.

"Really. Can I call you sometime?"

"I guess so. Or give me your number. I'll call you."

"I've got your number."

"How?"

The young man flinched for a moment then smiled as he came up with an answer. "The church. You work for the church. I'll call you there," he said. "By the way, my name is Roger."

"And I'm —"

"You're Gwen, Gwendolyn the queen." He took her hand and kissed it, then winked again before leaving.

OMG – Marcie mouthed as he left then burst out into a laugh.

"What's going on?" Gwen shook her head.

"I would say you are golden. It's about time men started to realize how amazing you are."

"No, something's not right. I suspect my mother is involved."

"Relax. Enjoy the attention. You deserve it."

"I do, don't I?" Gwen laughed. Still, what was her mother up to?

Chapter 6

"Hey, I thought I had July. What's going on here?" Bernice didn't wait for Laura to start the meeting.

"You do." Laura pulled out her poster board. "See, Bernice under July."

"Then what is Hattie doing sending in her guy before mine has his chance? I told you this wouldn't work."

"That is the rule. Hattie, you're supposed to wait till September."

"But my guy is too great to wait. Gwen is going to love him," Hattie said.

"Well, my Leon is every bit as great," Margie said. "So he's a little short. He and Gwen were lab partners in high school. I didn't even have to bribe him to get him to ask her out, unlike some people." Margie tipped her head toward Bernice.

"Wait, all three of you tried to set Gwen up with your man? No wonder my guy didn't have a chance," Laura said.

"You did too? I knew this was a bad idea," Bernice said.

"Hey, I'm her mother. I have a right to interfere in her life."

"And that you are," Hattie agreed.

"Look, you all have to back off. Gwen is getting suspicious. And you," Laura pointed at Bernice, "you had to bribe your guy? My daughter doesn't need bribery to get a date."

"Maybe a bad idea, still how has your way been working for her?" Bernice answered.

"She's very busy, hasn't had time for dating."

"Keep telling yourself that. We might as well give up," Bernice said.

"I didn't need to bribe my guy. All I had to do was show him Gwen's picture," Laura said.

"That and the Thunderbird," Hattie said.

"He did like that car," Laura admitted.

"You can't be promising that car to her date. That's not fair. We won't have a chance if you do that," Bernice said. "I told you this was a bad idea from the start."

"Lighten up, Bernice. Only if your guy can't win it for you," Laura said.

"Yeah, Bernice. Why do you have to be such a downer?" Margie added.

"Anyway, let's see what we can do to straighten out this mess. I say we go back to the plan. One month, one man."

"But our guys have already met Gwen. Won't she wonder if they wait a month before calling?" Hattie asked.

"And Leon's an old school chum. Why wouldn't he want to look her up? Gwen will get suspicious if he doesn't call," Margie said.

"She's already suspicious. Stick to the plan. Your guys can make up some excuse. Tell her they were called out of town on business."

"Your guy too?" Hattie asked Laura.

"Yes, my guy too," Laura said. "Now how about some cake?" With that Laura ended the meeting but she knew it wasn't over.

Chapter 7

Teens sat about the room, some lounged in bean bag chairs, others sat on the couch. Some were frowning as they waited for her to begin. Clearly, they didn't want to be there. Gwen could tell the youth group wasn't any happier about being assigned to her than she was to be assigned. It was just a step up from babysitting. Certainly, with all her years of study, she warranted more consideration. But no, youth group, a stepping stone to more meaningful ministry.

"You're the one stuck with us this time," a young woman with short, wavy, dark hair stated.

"I'm not stuck with you."

"Of course you are. Wouldn't you rather be talking to people closer to your age – adults? We know our place on the totem pole of church ministry. This year it's you. Next year it will be the next intern. No one likes to do youth group. Why should you be any different?" the young woman continued. Gwen didn't know how to respond. She had been thinking the same thing.

"Come on, Moira. Give her a chance," a young man standing in the back of the room spoke. "I'm Jacob Reese. I believe you know my family."

"I believe I do." Who didn't know the Reese family? The daughter, the infamous Kathleen, had married the pastor a year or so ago. The brother Dale was married to a teacher at the school, Ava. Gwen had been friends with Ava when she had been secretary. So this was Jacob? How quickly they grew. She remembered a skinny, gangly middle school boy, not this confidant young man. She heard he was a star player on the basketball team. Perhaps those dance classes as a child had helped. Now he was six foot something. He had grown into his body, though still not an adult. Had his brain caught up with his body yet?

"I remember you, but you've grown since I last saw you."

Jacob shrugged and looked away.

"And is that your sister Grace?" Gwen looked at the girl sharing the loveseat with another girl. She still had a small roll around her middle and a round face. She remembered Grace as being almost angelic. Now she was into the full pre-teen mode, with developing breasts, acne and braces.

"You remember me?" Grace asked.

"Sure I do."

"Do you remember my friend, Josie?"

"I don't believe we have met yet."

Where Grace was pudgy, her friend, Josie, was a slender reed. She appeared almost sickly and struggled to walk. Gwen had noticed it when Josie came into the room. She wondered what that was about. She made a mental note to ask Pastor Joe at their weekly meeting to discuss her progress.

Josie pushed back a strand of dark, black hair and politely stated, "Pleased to meet you."

"Come on. Let's get the introductions done so we can get onto planning our beach party," Moira interrupted the introductions. She would have to figure out how best to deal with this pesky teen at a later time. For now, they had an outing to plan.

Being in ministry meant wearing a lot of hats. Gwen knew this. It meant being chauffeur and event planner sometimes, as well as spiritual leader. How was she to get through the mundane to reach these children on a spiritual level? Something else to think about on those long nights alone in the manse.

Gwen figured getting a chauffeur's license was the least of her worries.

Chapter 8

Department of Motor Vehicles, DMV. Gwen looked at the listings on the inside of the building housing the police department and other offices. Didn't see it. The internet had said she could get a chauffer's license from the DMV. Where was it?

"Can I help you?" The voice of Officer Liam Kelley. How could she forget it?

She turned around to face the officer. He looked much older in his uniform, heavier too. Must have his bullet proof vest on. She made a mental note.

"I'm looking for the DMZ."

"The demilitarized zone?" Liam asked with a smile

"No, I'm sorry. The DMV, Department of Motor Vehicles." Gwen could feel her face turn red with embarrassment. "I came to apply for a chauffeur's license."

"Then you want the Secretary of State. That's down the corridor to the left." Liam pointed her in the right direction.

"Thanks," Gwen stated. She struggled to come up with something to redeem herself. Some charming bit of conversation. Nothing came to mind as she stood awkwardly in the hallway.

"Good luck," Liam said.

"With what?"

"Your application."

"Oh, yeah, that." Gwen had almost forgotten what she had come here for. "Well, thank you." Gwen backed away, her eyes still focused on him, till she backed up into another body. "I'm so sorry," she told the man then turned back to see Liam still smiling at her. "Maybe I'll see you again sometime."

"Maybe," Liam said with a smile then walked away.

"Maybe," Gwen repeated to herself. Maybe, she smiled.

How hard could it be to get a chauffer's license? She had checked it out online, watched a YouTube video on it. All she had to do was pass the written exam and pay the fee. No test drive. Easy-peasy. Of course she needed to go to the right place. Who'd have thought there was no DMV in Michigan?

She walked into the Secretary of State and lost her smile. The place was packed with people. Teens clutching learning permits, seniors requesting handicap plates, others getting plates for boats and license renewals. She figured she was looking at all morning before getting done. She stood in one line then was told to go take a seat and wait her turn.

When her number came up, she went up to the open window. "I'm here to get a chauffeur's license."

"And why do you need a chauffeur's license?" the woman stared down her glasses and asked.

"Because my boss told me I needed one."

"You need to be more specific." The woman sighed.

"Because I need it to drive the church van."

"How many people does the van hold?"

"Twelve, I think. Does it matter?"

"Yes, because if it holds sixteen or more you need a CDL."

"CDL?"

"Yes."

"I don't even know what a CDL is."

"Commercial Driving License."

"Look, all Pastor Joe told me was I need a chauffer's license."

"Pastor Joe? Why didn't you say so? You must be the new intern."

"How do you know?"

"Because every year he sends someone here for a chauffer's license. First it was volunteer youth ministers. Now that he has an intern, he sends them. I tell him he should get one himself. That's what I have interns for, he tells me." She handed some papers to

Gwen. "You don't need a CDL to drive the church van. Just complete the application and take the test."

Gwen took the written exam and went back to fill it out. She filled it out, passed with the required number of right answers and paid for her license. Easy-peasy.

Chapter 9

The sun beat down on the sand. Gwen could feel the heat coming up through the blanket she had spread out. She pulled her swimsuit cover-up off over her head. The perfect day to work on her tan, she thought as she rubbed sunscreen on her skin. Maybe youth ministry wasn't so bad. She had managed to make it here safely with a van full of teens. Dale and Ava Reese, the chaperones, had come in their own car. She had a cooler full of pop and water sitting next to her, bags of chips and Doritos to stave off hungry teens made ravenous by hours in the water. Dale and Ava were going to pick up pizza for the group once they were done swimming. Easy-peasy. Then all she had to do was get the wet, sandy group back to the church into the waiting arms of their parents and clean out the van.

She surveyed the group of teens, then discreetly scanned for any men her age. Sun glasses were great for this. The beach was populated primarily with families. No single men her age that she could see. She sighed and went back to checking on her teen charges. The girls laid on the dock in bikinis, soaking up rays and talking until splashed by the boys. Hormones were rampant. Was this really a good idea, she wondered to herself as she watched. Exposing teen-age boys to those bodies? Some of the boys were throwing girls off the dock into the water. They screamed and protested but didn't seem too upset. The younger teens kept to themselves. Grace and her friend Josie walked along the edge of the beach, looking for shells. Grace patiently stayed by her friend's side. Again she wondered, was this a good idea as Josie struggled to walk among the sand and stones. But then, it hadn't been her decision. The decision had been made for her, before she got there.

Ava and Dale came up beside her and placed folding lounge chairs next to her blanket. They were sipping out of large plastic containers. Gwen regretted not bringing her own cup with maybe a bit of vodka and orange juice? No, not at a church function, no matter how lame.

Once Dale and Ava were firmly planted by her side, she rolled over on her stomach, allowing the sun to bake her back side while they kept an eye on the kids.

"Gwen? Is that you?"

Gwen rolled over. The sun glared behind the figure standing over her. She lifted her sunglasses to get a better look. She recognized the glasses and short dark hair. Leon. "Leon, what are you doing here?"

"Just enjoying the sun. What about you?"

"I'm here with the youth group from church."

"What a coincidence. You here. Me here. Why haven't you called me yet?"

"Sorry. I've been busy, learning a new job and all."

"No worry. Mind if I sit down?" Leon sat down on her blanket before she had a chance to tell him she minded. He removed his t-shirt, revealing a scrawny chest with a patch of dark hair and a slight paunch. Gwen looked away. Again she was happy for her sunglasses and the protection they afforded. She sat up and put on a floppy beach hat.

Leon introduced himself to Dale and Ava. "We know each other from high school," he explained without being asked.

"Gwen?"

"Gordon?" Gwen was surprised by the other man from the Crab Shack.

"It's good to see you. You haven't answered my calls. I was beginning to think you had moved away."

"No, just busy."

"Gwen?" Yet another voice beckoned. "What a surprise seeing you here. I was just thinking about you."

"Roger?"

"Yes, from Burger Barn. You remember, of course. How could you not remember me?"

"How could I?" Gwen said with a sigh.

Gordon stepped in front of Roger and pulled off his shirt to reveal a buffed, tanned muscular chest. "Gwen, you don't mind if I share your blanket with you, do you?"

As if on cue, Roger removed his shirt as well.

"I do mind," Gwen finally managed to spit out. "I'm here working. I'm supposed to be with the church youth group."

"They seem to be doing just fine." Gordon looked out over the beach at the teens.

"But I'm not, fine that is. What do I have to do to get you to leave?"

"Simple. Agree to go out with me," Gordon said.

"Fine. I will. Call me."

"So you can keep putting me off? I want a time and day."

"Okay. Coffee, Saturday morning."

"How about dinner, Saturday night? I insist."

"All right. Whatever it takes," Gwen agreed.

"That means I get Friday," Roger said.

"Yes, fine, whatever. Now will you let me get back to my job?"

Both left. Roger turned around and motioned with his hands about calling him. Gwen chose to ignore him.

"The nerve of some people," Leon said as they left.

"You need to leave too, Leon."

"I won't cause any trouble. I'll just sit here quietly and gaze at you." Leon gave her what he apparently thought was an endearing smile.

"Leon, go. Get out of here," Gwen said.

"But I didn't get a date."

"Fine. When?"

"Sunday night?"

"Whatever. Now will you leave?"

"Yes!" Leon squeezed his hand into a fist and shook it triumphantly before leaving.

"That was something to watch," Ava commented after the men had left. "I didn't know you were so popular."

"Neither did I. Or, I'm not. Something's just not right," Gwen said.

"Or maybe these men are just now realizing how attractive you are," Ava said.

"Not likely."

"You are pretty, Gwen. Don't you realize that?" Ava persisted.

"I don't know. I guess. I never thought that much about it. I never thought of myself as a leading lady type. I've always been more of a sidekick. You know, comic relief." She had been Marcie's side kick for so long. It didn't seem possible she could be anyone else.

"You tell her, Dale."

"Tell her what?" Dale had used the cover of sunglasses to sneak in a few zzzzs. He shook himself awake.

"Tell her how pretty she is, and smart, and fun to be with. Any man would be lucky to date her."

"Is this a trap?" Dale smiled as he carefully chose his words. "Because, you know, I only have eyes for you, dear."

"Dale, tell her."

"It won't get me in trouble?"

"Why would the truth get you in trouble?"

"You tell me."

Ava continued to stare down Dale until he finally answered.

"All right. Gwen, you are pretty. In fact, you are gorgeous. And you have a great personality. Any man who can't see that is a fool." He turned to face Ava. "Satisfied now?"

"That depends. Gwen, do you believe him?"

Gwen laughed. "Maybe someday I'll have a relationship like yours."

"Oh, dear, you can do so much better," Ava teased.

"Hey?" Dale said.

Ava smiled and reached for Dale's hand. "Just you and me kid."

"That's right." He smiled, laughed and kissed her. Their laughter was interrupted by shouts from the lake shore.

"Vicar Gwen!" one of the youth group yelled. "Something's wrong with Carrie. Come quick." One of the boys was struggling to hold Carrie up.

Gwen looked about. Where was the rest of the group? She saw Grace and Josie, but some of the boys were missing. "I'll be right there," she called out. Gwen kicked off her sandals and ran through the hot sand to the dock and dove into the water. Dale and Ava followed her down to the edge of the water. Her face hit sand. She had forgotten how shallow the water was, even off the dock. She surfaced, gasped for air and shook her head then swam to where Carrie was being supported by the boy.

She stood up in the chest deep water and put her arm around Carrie. "What's the problem?"

"I've got cramps in my side," Carrie said.

"Can you walk?"

"I guess so, with help." Carrie yelled out in pain and bent over, holding her side.

"What's your name?" Gwen asked the boy who had been holding Carrie up.

"Trevor."

"Okay, Trevor. You take one side and I'll take the other. Do you think you can do that? We'll walk Carrie to the shore."

It was slow going, with Carrie bending over in pain every two or three steps, but they finally reached the shore where Dale and Ava waited. Ava wrapped Carrie in a towel and helped her to the blanket.

"Are you okay now?" Ava asked.

"Yes. I'm fine. I don't know what came over me," Carrie said. Ava pulled a bottle of water out of the cooler and gave it to Carrie.

"You stay here," Gwen said. "I'll go over and see what we have in the van." Gwen looked where the van had been parked and realized it was gone.

"The van!" Gwen reached into her beach bag where she had hidden the keys. No keys. "It's gone. Someone must have taken the keys while I was in the water. What are we going to do?"

"Don't worry," Dale said. "I've called the police. Someone will be here shortly."

"You called the police?" Carrie said. "Why did you do that?"

"Because someone stole the church van," Dale stated. By then the rest of the youth group had gathered around the blanket. Gwen did a head count and realized she was missing two members.

"No need to tell me who's missing," Dale said. "Jacob and Alex."

"Carrie, what do you know about this?" Ava quizzed the girl.

"It was just a joke," Carrie confessed. "I was supposed to pretend to have a cramp to distract you so Jacob and Alex could find your keys and move the van. They were just going to move it. Just enough to freak you out. No one was supposed to call the cops."

"Well, my son failed to inform me about his joke. Where is the van now?"

"I don't know. Honest. It was all Jacob's idea," Carrie said.

"No surprise there." Dale looked over at Ava. Ava was busy handing out pop and passing around the bag of chips to shivering, towel-wrapped teens.

"How are we getting home, Mrs. Reese?" one of the teens asked Ava.

"Don't worry. We'll get the van back," Gwen assured them.

"I called my dad," another said. "He's coming to get me."

"There's no reason to call your parents," Gwen said.

Too late. Multiple cell phones were already calling home.

"This is a disaster," Gwen said to Dale and Ava.

"Maybe it's just as well they go home with their parents. The police are going to want a full report," Dale said.

Just then, a police car pulled up, followed by the church van. Jacob and Alex sat in the back of the police car.

Gwen cringed when she saw Officer Kelley get out of the van. Both officers approached the group with Jacob and Alex in between them.

"No cuffs?" Dale asked.

"Didn't think we needed them. However, that could be arranged," the first officer said.

Officer Kelley handed Gwen the keys to the church van. "This why you needed the chauffeur's license?"

"Yes." Gwen accepted the keys and put them back in the beach bag. Suddenly she was all too aware of how little clothes she had on. She reached for a towel and wrapped it around her to hide her bikini-clad body.

"Do you want to press charges?" the first officer asked.

"No, er, I don't think so." Gwen looked to Dale for confirmation.

"Don't worry, officer. By the time I get done with my son, he'll wish you had taken him in and booked him. I expect it will be the same for Alex here," Dale said.

Parents started to arrive and gather their children. They glared at Gwen as she tried to explain.

"We can still get pizza," she said as the teens were led away.

"It's okay, Gwen. This will blow over," Ava assured her.

"Like twenty years from now. Pastor Joe will never forgive me."

"Don't worry about Pastor Joe. We'll explain everything," Ava said while Dale filled Alex's parents in on what had happened. Soon, the only teens left were Jacob, Grace and Josie.

"Did you want to ride with me?" Gwen asked.

"That's okay. We'll drop Josie off at her home," Dale told her. "And you, young man, don't you have something to say to Gwen?"

"I'm sorry," Jacob shrugged and attempted a smile. "It was just supposed to be a joke. We always play jokes on the youth minister. I guess this went too far."

"You are right there, son. It'll be a long time before you are out of our sight long enough to try another stunt like this."

Gwen could tell that Jacob was going to feel even sorrier by the time Dale doled out his punishment. There was no comfort in the thought.

"Look on the bright side." Ava placed her hand on Gwen's shoulder. "At least you don't have to ride back with eleven wet and sandy teens in the van, so now you won't have to clean it."

"For some reason that doesn't help," Gwen told her. She picked up the cooler and the empty chip bags and drove back to the church. The news of what had happened most likely had preceded her. No comfort in that thought either.

Chapter 10

Laura sat in her T-bird in the cove overlooking the beach, binoculars in one hand, a milk shake in the other. She sipped as she watched the events of the afternoon unfold.

"What do you think you're doing here?" Hattie opened the passenger side door and sat down. She was followed by Bernice and Margie, climbing into the back seat. "You two here too?" Hattie asked.

"We just followed you – right, Bernice?" Margie said.

"What does it look like I'm doing?" Laura said, ignoring the intervening conversation. "I'm enjoying a milk shake and the view."

"And spying on your daughter. Not a good idea. She'll find out and the whole game will be over," Bernice added.

"What? Gwen's here?"

"You know that. Gwen's here with the youth group," Hattie said.

"Oh, that. Yes, there she is. I suppose you came to see how your guys are doing."

"I thought we had an agreement," Bernice pulled herself up between the two in the front seat. "You were supposed to call your guys off. This won't work if you don't follow the rules. I knew all along this wasn't going to work."

"Looks like someone didn't get the message," Laura said as she gazed through the binoculars.

"What are you talking about?" Hattie asked.

"I see these partially clad men, strutting their stuff for Gwen."

"Let me have those binoculars." Bernice grabbed the binoculars from Laura and peered through them. "I don't see them."

"Here, try these." Hattie pulled binoculars out of her purse and handed them to Bernice. Bernice handed Laura's back to her. Laura looked over at Hattie and asked without saying a word.

"Bird watching. You never know when you'll see something interesting. I carry them with me all the time," Hattie explained.

Laura lowered her binoculars and raised her eyebrows. "Like I'm going to believe that."

"Hey, what about me?" Margie pulled forward. Bernice passed the binoculars to her.

"My guy's on the blanket with Gwen," she said as she peered through the glasses. "That's more than you can say."

"Let me have those binoculars." Hattie grabbed them from Margie. "Yeah, but it looks like Gwen is giving all of them the bum's rush, even Leon." Hattie put the binoculars down and passed them back to Bernice.

"Did anyone bring any food?" Margie asked.

"Here, have some trail mix." Laura handed a bag of trail mix back to Margie while still holding on to her binoculars.

"There's no M&M's in this. What kind of trail mix doesn't have M&M's?"

"The healthy kind. There's raisins and other dried fruit," Laura answered.

"It's not the same." Margie reached into the bag for more.

"What's happening now?" Bernice peered through the binoculars. "It looks like something's wrong. Someone's drowning."

"Let me see." Hattie grabbed the binoculars from Bernice.

"That's my girl. She's running to the rescue. Look at her dive in — ouch." Laura shook her head.

"Doesn't she know it's too shallow for diving off the dock, even a racing dive?" Hattie passed the binoculars back to Bernice.

"She does now," Laura said. "She's okay. It looks like one of the kids is having a problem. Gwen's helping her get to shore. That's my girl."

"What are those boys doing with Gwen's bag?" Bernice asked.

"What boys?" Laura looked back up the beach and saw two boys take something out of her daughter's bag then run for the parking lot. "Looks like they took her keys."

"What now? Is the girl all right?" Hattie asked.

"It looks like it. She's sitting on the blanket," Laura said. "Oh, it looks like they just noticed the van is gone."

"Let me see," Margie asked from the back. Bernice passed the binoculars to her. "Mmmm, chips. Why didn't we bring chips?"

"Is that all you think about? Gwen is in trouble and surely will end up in jail and all you can think about is food," Bernice said.

"I can't help it. I'm hungry."

"Let me have those binoculars back. What's happening now?" Hattie raised the binoculars to her eyes.

"The police are there, followed by the church van," Laura said. "Two of the boys are getting out of the police car. Another officer is getting out of the van."

"Busted, like I said," Bernice said.

Laura watched as one by one angry parents arrived and picked up their kids.

"Looks like Gwen's in trouble," Margie said.

"She is," Laura agreed, "but we aren't going to say anything, right? She must never know we were here. As far as she knows, we were just joy-riding in the Thunderbird if she asks us what we were doing today."

"That's right," Hattie said.

"They're gone." Laura lowered her binoculars. Hattie put hers back in her purse.

"Poor Gwen," Bernice said. All four sat there in silence.

"What can we do?" Margie wondered out loud.

"Not much we can do from up here." Hattie shook her head.

"It's sad though. I wish there was something we could do. I told you no good would come from this," Bernice said.

"Always hard when our kids hurt." Hattie sighed. "But sometimes you just have to let them fall so they can pick themselves back up. Right?"

Laura slurped her milk shake.

"Anyone else hungry?" Margie asked.

"I am," Bernice said.

"I'm a might peckish myself," Hattie agreed. "A burger sounds good. What about you, Laura? You want to join us?"

"No, I'm okay," Laura said.

"Where to, ladies? Burger Barn?" Hattie said.

"Sounds good to me," Margie said.

"Me too. See you there." All three climbed out of the Thunderbird.

"You sure you're all right?" Hattie asked Laura.

"I'm fine. I've got my milk shake and trail mix."

"You had trail mix," Margie said.

"Whatever. I'll enjoy the view a while longer then head for home. Have to fix Walter something to eat."

Laura finished off her milk shake with a loud slurp then backed out of the spot and cruised down the highway, the top down and the wind blowing through her hair as her mind worked.

Chapter 11

Gwen pushed her way through overgrown bushes and weeds, hiding the sidewalk to the house. Did she have the right place? She hadn't been able to find a house number. Was this the right door? She didn't see any other path to another door.

Pastor Joe had said surprisingly little about the incident at Otter Lake when they met earlier that week.

"Sometimes these things happen," was all he said. "The parents will get over it."

"Will they?"

"They know what teens are like. They know about pranks as well. They probably pulled a few in their day."

"Did you?"

"Did I what?"

"Pull a few pranks as a teen?"

"This is about you, not me."

"I'm just wondering if there was a less than perfect teen under your minister façade."

Pastor Joe laughed at this. "Not one I'm going to let you know about."

It felt good to laugh with the Pastor. Made him feel more like a peer, and her, less like the lowly church secretary she once was. When he laughed, he was an ally in ministry. She liked that.

She rapped on the door, her mind returning to the present. Pastor Joe had given her the address for this, her first pastoral visit.

A small old woman with hair pulled back in a bun, wearing a baggy dress over her skinny frame, opened the door.

"Come in," a male voice called from another room. The woman led the way to the kitchen where a middle-aged man lay on a hospital bed. Gwen's nose was assaulted by odors she couldn't quite place. Similar to the smells of the street people she had served in

Chicago. But not the same. The smell of decay. The man was as happy to see her as the woman was morose. His hair hung about his face in long, lank brown strands. Why had Pastor Joe sent her here?

"Sit down," the man commanded. Gwen looked for a place to sit. There were stacks of newspapers and magazines cluttering the table, the counter and every chair. "Ma, clear a place for the minister."

The woman picked up a stack of newspapers and sat them on top of another stack, leaving a kitchen chair free for sitting. Gwen sat down on the edge of the chair.

"Come closer," the man demanded. Gwen slid the chair closer to the hospital bed. "Would you like something to drink? Ma, get the minister something to drink."

"No, no thank you," Gwen insisted. "I'm not thirsty."

"Very well then. Ma," he called again. She brought over a glass with a straw and held it up to his lips for him to sip. "Thanks, Ma." He nodded his head to indicate that was enough.

"I'm Richard Dalton. I've got MS. I expect the Pastor has already told you that."

"He didn't tell me much."

"Wants me to tell you, I guess."

"I guess." Gwen shifted in the chair, trying to get comfortable.

"I was an airline pilot. Flew jets over the Middle East while in the air force. Then commercial airlines out of Kuwait. Pay was better than in the states. But those Muslims, crazy. I had to teach them how to fly planes. One time when the plane was going to crash, the Muslim threw up his hands and said, 'Allah will provide!' Like hell he will, I told him and took over the controls. Crazy. I flew until MS made it impossible. But God is curing me. Did Pastor Joe tell you that?"

"No, he didn't."

"God told me in a dream. I've got all these natural foods and vitamins. But one night, I dreamt I was sitting at a table, a big feast spread out before me. All my favorite foods. Roast beef, mashed potatoes and gravy, green bean casserole, when a voice sounded like thunder and said, 'NO SALT!' Woke up right out of a sound sleep. It had to be God speaking. No salt, the voice said. I haven't had a hint of salt since that day. I also cut out MSG. Looked it up. Not good for you." He reached up and itched his nose with a fingernail that extended two times the length of the part of the nail still attached to his finger.

"God is going to heal me, already is. Another time, I dreamed I was walking again. But that voice. It was as loud and plain as you sitting right there." Richard took a breath. "Tell me about yourself."

"Not much to tell."

"You married?"

"No."

"Young men, they're fools. A pretty girl like you should have plenty of suitors."

"You think?"

"I know."

"From your lips to God's ear," Gwen teased.

"Precisely," Richard responded. "You'll see."

They chatted for a while then Gwen asked if he would like her to say a prayer over him. Always ask, she had been instructed in her unit of CPE – Clinical Pastoral Education. Don't presume that everyone wants you to pray over them. For some people it can feel like a violation of their sacred space. Especially when visiting people in the hospital. They have already been stripped of so many aspects of their humanity, their clothes, their privacy. Doctors, nurses, hospital staff, visitors come in any time they want. Afford them the opportunity to say no, unless you have a relationship with them such that you know they are okay with you praying over them or had been given permission on a previous visit. Even then, you may need to ask. Just because it's okay one time, doesn't mean it's okay the next time. The same was true for touch. Don't presume to touch anyone without permission. That too can be construed as a violation. Over time you may develop a sense for when a person wants prayer and whether to hold their hand or place your hand on their head. But when in doubt, ask she had been instructed. Gwen felt she was a long way from developing that intuition.

When Richard said he would like prayer, Gwen bowed her head and prayed for healing and peace of mind. She also prayed for his mother and her role as caretaker. When she was done, she raised her head and saw him staring at her.

"Something wrong?" she asked.

"No, nothing. What you said was perfect." Gwen doubted that. Her words had felt so insufficient; she felt inadequate for what she was doing. She guessed God had provided and Richard heard what he needed to hear.

She thought about how she had ended up in this situation as she drove home. She had never considered herself a potential minister, until she did. Senior year in college. She had been at a loss about what to do with her life and had experienced "the call" as some referred to it.

"When did you receive your call?" she was always asked in seminary. She didn't know. It wasn't like God picked up the phone and punched in her number. It had not been a call so much as an inclination, a nudge. She had never been that religious, had not attended church on a regular basis until she started working as church secretary at the beginning of her senior year in college. Even then, even now, she wondered. Had she made the right choice? Or was it just the chance to get away from her mother and her drama? There were other means of leaving, other grad schools she could have attended. Or she could have gotten a job somewhere, anywhere, as long as it wasn't Cascade Falls. And if she wanted out so badly, why did she come back? Another question for which she didn't know the answer.

Her dad had asked her the same question. She had come over to see how he was doing and found him on the patio sipping iced tea.

"Iced tea? Really, Dad. Since when do you drink iced tea?"

"No more of the hard stuff for me. Or, only in moderation, extreme moderation."

"Where's Mom?"

"Off somewhere with her friends, probably joy riding in her Thunderbird."

"Leaving you alone?"

"I'm not an invalid, Gwen. Many men my age, given my stress level and work load, have heart attacks and make full recoveries."

"I know Dad."

"Then why are you here?"

"Can't I visit my dad without there being a reason? Isn't wanting to see you reason enough?"

"I'm always happy to see you, but moving back here when all you ever wanted was to move away and never come back? That wasn't exactly the plan. Why? And don't say because of me, my heart attack."

"Other men who have had heart attacks did not have Mom to deal with."

"Is this about your mom, then, not me?"

"Maybe. I don't know."

"Your mom is doing great, better than ever. She has friends, her work, her Thunderbird."

"I know, but …"

"But what?"

"That was before she had to deal with your heart attack. I didn't know how she would handle it."

"She's handling it just fine. We're both fine. But your mom is glad you're here. She'd love to have you move back here permanently."

"Don't I know. Not going to happen. Once I'm ordained, I'll be assigned as associate to another church. The denomination likes its ministers to get a variety of experiences."

"St. Luke's could use an associate."

"Not you too, Dad. Why did I come home if I have to put up with this?"

"Because you love your dear old dad and want him to be happy."

"That I do." Gwen placed a kiss on his cheek then looked at her phone. "Time to get back to the church."

"Come back any time," her dad shouted as she let herself out.

Why did she come back? She found herself wondering this as she drove back to church. If her dad didn't need her, then why had she felt the need to return?

Chapter 12

Gwen thought there was nothing her mom could do that would surprise her. She was wrong. She was surprised when her mom showed up at the manse with a massive brown dog.

"If you insist on living here alone instead of at home, then you need someone to keep you safe. Sam here is the perfect solution. He'll protect you and keep you company."

"Mom, if I wanted a dog, I'm perfectly capable of choosing my own."

"But Sam here is a rescue. If no one took him he would be put to sleep. You don't want that to happen to him. Just look at his face. How could you say no to such a face?" Her mom reached down and held Sam's face. Sam drooled in response.

"Easy. No. If you think he's so cute, you take him. What kind of dog is he anyway?"

"A mastiff. You know your dad can't have a dog. He's allergic."

"How convenient."

Her mom squatted down next to Sam, rubbing his back. "He's a great man-magnet, you know."

Gwen felt her phone vibrate. She recognized the number. Roger. Ooops, she had forgotten about their date.

"Hey, baby, you running late? You want me to pick you up?" his voice sounded through her phone.

"No, no. That's okay. I'm leaving right now. Where are we meeting?" Gwen had not wanted to be picked up for the date. If it went bad, she wanted to be able to go home without Roger. One dinner, then she would be done with him.

"You got a date?" her mom asked.

"Yes, I do."

"Anyone I know?"

"I don't think so. Mom, what are you going to do with Sam?"

"I can't take him home and I can't take him back to the pound. It's too late." Sam laid his head down on his paws and stared up at Gwen with his big brown eyes.

"I don't care what you do. Just do something. I've got to go." Gwen hopped into her car and drove off, leaving her mom with the dog. She looked back at the two, then backed up.

"All right. He can stay tonight. He is house-broken, isn't he?"

"I think so."

"If he isn't, you'll be the one to answer to Pastor Joe about it when he ruins the carpet. Go ahead, let him in. Do you have dog food?"

"Dog food and chew toys. Don't worry. I'll take care of everything. You have a good time on your date."

At least the dog will give her an excuse to leave early, she thought as she drove to the restaurant. Roger had picked one of the nicer restaurants in Cascade Falls. Not some chain restaurant sitting on the outskirts of town with other chain restaurants and hotels. A nice Italian restaurant, a little pricey for her budget, but she wasn't paying. She might as well enjoy herself.

Roger was already seated when she got there. He waved at her, then stood up and held her chair for her.

"I've already ordered us a bottle of wine. I hope you don't mind. You do drink, don't you? You being a minister and all?"

"On occasion."

"Then let's make this one of those special occasions. The first of many." Roger lifted his glass in a toast then took a sip.

Roger also ordered appetizers, seafood – mussels, shrimp, calamari. Gwen ordered a simple pasta. She didn't want to be too extravagant on a first date. Roger ordered steak pizzaioli. The evening was going much better than she had expected. She almost regretted not letting him pick her up. He was charming and funny, until …

"That was the summer after the alien abduction."

"What?" Gwen shook her head, thinking she hadn't heard right.

"The alien abduction. They took me to their ship and probed me. I think they left some type of transmitter inside me. Like a radio receiver. Every now and then I hear these strange alien voices. They came back and took me to their mother ship. You should go sometime. It's really awesome inside that ship. Then all those little alien creatures. They're not tall and slender like you see on some movies. They're little, more like little ETs running around. And they don't talk, not like we do. They transmit words telepathically, right into your brain."

"Are they saying something now?"

"Let me see." Roger put his fingers on either side of his temple and squinted. "Nah, nothing."

"Would you care for dessert?" the waiter asked.

"None for me," Gwen said.

"Are you sure? I've heard their tiramisu is out of this world," Roger said.

"You ought to know," Gwen said under her breath. "No, no, in fact I need to get home. I've got to let my dog out. But you have dessert if you want to. I'll find my way out."

"Are you sure, because, you and me, you know, we've got this vibe going on." He pointed at her then back at himself. "I can tell. I mean, I think we've got something good here."

"I've got to go." Gwen prepared to stand up.

"Okay, then. Waiter, the check." Roger called to the waiter. "Do you suppose you could lend me a hundred bucks?" he leaned over and whispered. "Just until payday."

"I don't carry that kind of money around."

"Oh, then that's a problem."

"You mean you can't pay the bill?"

"Not without your hundred dollars."

Gwen dug into her purse, pulled out her credit card and gave it to the waiter.

"Hey, this has been great. When can we do this again?" Roger said.

Gwen signed the bill and put her credit card back in her purse. "You know those radio transmitters in your head? See if you can receive what I'm thinking."

"No, I'm not getting anything."

"Let's see if this helps." Gwen looked around the restaurant to make sure no one was watching then leaned over and held up one hand to cover the other as she extended her finger in a crude gesture. "Never again," Gwen mumbled on her way out.

She had forgotten about Sam until she put the key in her door and heard growling. "Sam, it's me. It's okay. I live here. Let me in." Sam's response was to start barking. She went over to the window to see what he was doing. Sam jumped at the window with teeth bared.

Worst night ever, she thought as she called her mom. "Mom, Sam won't let me in."

"What am I supposed to do about it?"

"Sam, the dog you got me. He won't let me in. He's growling and snarling."

"That's because he doesn't know you yet. Don't worry. Once he gets to know you, he'll be slobbering kisses all over you."

"I know that, Mom. But until that happens, you get over here and help me out." Gwen tried going to the back door. Sam was there waiting, growling in the kitchen.

"Are you sure this dog isn't Kujo?" Gwen asked her mom when she arrived.

"He's a sweet dog. Just think how safe you'll feel with him guarding your house."

"If I can ever get inside."

Her mom went up to the front door. "Sam," she called. "Remember me? I'm the lady who rescued you from the pound." She started to open the door. Sam lunged at her. She slammed the door shut. "We have to figure out something."

"He doesn't remember you."

"Apparently not." Laura peered into the window.

"What if we lure him out with a big bone?"

"That could work."

They went to the meat department of their local grocery store and found a large soup bone.

"Okay, we go to the door, show him the bone. Then we open the door, throw the bone, run inside and close the door before he gets back," Laura said.

"You lure him out."

"Me? Why do I have to? He's your dog."

"Mom." Gwen stared her down.

"All right. You get behind me on the porch. Get ready to run."

"Something wrong, ladies?" They hadn't noticed a police car pull up. "I received a call about something suspicious at St. Luke's manse. That wouldn't be you, would it?"

Gwen gulped. Officer Kelley again.

"That would be us. We're the suspicious activity. I mean, this is my house, or where I live, but I can't get in."

"Locked out?"

"No, my dog. He won't let us in."

"Your dog?"

"It was my mom's idea." Her mom waved from behind Gwen. "She got Sam from the pound. Thought I needed a dog to protect me, but now he won't let me in."

"Sam, a big mastiff?"

"That would be him. Do you know him?"

"Yes, if it's the same dog. How did he end up in the pound?"

"I don't know. I just know now he's in my home and he won't let me in. We were going to try to lure him out with this bone."

"Let me try. Mastiffs are great dogs. Real friendly. You just have to know how to talk to them." Officer Kelley went up to the door and opened it. "Here boy, here Sam." Sam ran up to Officer Kelley and started licking him. "That's a good boy." Officer Kelley scratched Sam's jowls and rubbed his belly.

"Sam used to belong to an old man on my beat. Last I knew the man had died. I didn't know what happened to Sam. We had him at the precinct for a while till arrangements were made. Thought maybe the man's daughter had taken him. What do you want me to do? I can take Sam back to the precinct if you want me to, but once he gets to know you, he'll be a great dog."

"I don't know." Gwen hesitated.

"You can start by giving him that big bone."

Gwen walked over to Sam and gave him the bone.

"There now, see how friendly he is," Officer Kelley said.

Gwen reached over to pet him. Sam growled.

"He thinks you're trying to take his bone. Here, scratch him right above his tail. He loves that."

Gwen scratched him. Sam made guttural sounds of pleasure while still gnawing the bone.

"See. He's warming up to you already." Officer Kelley stepped aside to respond to his radio. "I've got another call. What do you want me to do about Sam? Should I take him with me?"

"No, I guess not. We just got off on the wrong paw, right Sam?" Gwen said, reaching down and rubbing him.

"If you have any more problems, give me a call." He started to hand Gwen a card.

"I've already got your card."

"That's right, from the Crab Shack. We seem to be seeing a lot of each other." Officer Kelley tipped his hat and started to leave.

"Thank you, Officer," Laura shouted after him. "He's cute," she said to Gwen as soon as Officer Kelley was out of sight.

"Yeah, well, let's hope I don't have to call him any more tonight, right Sam?" Sam continued to gnaw happily on his bone.

"By the way, how did your date go?" her mom asked.

"Beam me up, Scotty. He was waiting for the mother ship."

"That bad?"

"Worse. He stuck me with the bill."

"Then I guess he's out." Laura shook her head.

"Out of what?"

"Out of his mind. Anyone would have to be out of their mind to treat you that way, as adorable as you are."

"Yeah, right, Mom. Go on home. Me and Sam, we have some TV to watch." Gwen grabbed Sam by the collar and pulled him into the living room where he jumped on the couch with his bone, leaving barely any room for Gwen.

Chapter 13

Another lame date, Gwen thought as she drove to Crab Shack. Maybe she could leave early. Use Sam as an excuse. Gwen didn't want to go out on another date after last night's fiasco, but she didn't know how to get out of it. She had promised.

She parked and was about to go into the Crab Shack when she heard her name called.

"Gwen! Gwen! Over here!" Gordon was standing on a dock.

"I thought we were going to the Crab Shack," Gwen stated as she crossed the road to the pier.

"This is better. We're having a picnic." Gordon helped her off the dock onto a large pontoon. He untied the boat and pushed off from the dock.

"A picnic? Did you fix it?"

"My aunt did. It was her idea. Fried chicken, homemade potato salad, brownies, and a bottle of wine. The wine was my idea." Gordon pulled out a bottle of red wine and two wine glasses from the picnic basket. "Care for some Cabernet?" He pulled out the cork and poured a glass for Gwen then one for himself. Then he sat down at the helm and pulled out onto the lake. "Nice, isn't it?"

"It is," Gwen admitted. She peered over her wine glass at his bronze body, exposed under a white tank top and khaki shorts. She relaxed as the boat floated across the lake. Water had that effect on her. Water and wine. Maybe this would be a good date after all. Gordon found a spot to put down anchor where they could watch the sunset while they ate their dinner.

The chicken was fried to perfection, crispy, not greasy. Homemade potato salad, not drenched in mayonnaise. Just the way she liked it. And brownies. Need she say more? A little bit of heaven.

They clinked glasses as multiple shades of pink spread across the horizon.

"So, this is your boat?" Gwen asked.

"It might as well be."

"What do you mean?"

"It's my uncle's. I stay here for free as long as I take care of it. Clean it, take care of repairs, you know. There's a lot of work to keeping up a boat."

"You stay here? You mean you use it, right?"

"No, I live here. This is my home when I'm in Cascade Falls. I keep my clothes stashed under the seat. And that seat," he pointed at the one Gwen was sitting on that ran the length of the back of the boat. "That is my bed. You, my lady, are in my bedroom."

Gwen squirmed and moved to another seat. "What do you do in winter? You can't stay here."

"Of course not, silly. I put the boat in storage."

"You stay in the storage unit?" Gwen almost didn't ask. She wasn't sure she wanted to hear the answer.

"Sometimes, when I'm not sleeping on my friend Boomer's couch."

"Boomer?"

"Yeah. He's a great guy. We're going to meet him later at the Crab Shack. Unless, of course, this evening takes a romantic turn. If you know what I mean."

"Oh, I know." Gwen shivered at the thought. She should have known better than to allow herself to be trapped on a boat out in the middle of the lake. Fortunately, the shore wasn't too far away. She could swim for it if she had to. Gwen slid further away from Gordon.

"What do you do besides take care of this boat?"

"I'm working on my tan," Gordon responded.

"I see that. You have quite a tan."

"No, I'm working on it. You have no idea how hard it is to get a perfect tan."

"Tell me about it." Gwen grimaced when he took her seriously and began to expound on the subject.

"I mean, you have to watch out for those tan lines. If this were day light, I couldn't wear this shirt."

"Tan lines?"

"Right. Same thing for shoes. I go barefoot as often as I can, and when I can't—"

"—Sandals," Gwen interjected.

"That's right. You get me. I never met a girl who gets me like you do. And, you know, for the private parts." Gordon started to pull his shorts down.

"Please don't show me."

Gordon pulled them back up. "I wear speedos. Exposes everything except —"

Gwen stopped him. "That's enough. I get it. But what do you do for money?"

"I don't need much, living here on the boat. And, when I get that perfect tan, I'll be in demand as a model. I've got to keep in shape. That's why I didn't eat any brownies."

"I wondered."

"My aunt said that you liked them. That's why she made them. I can't risk getting fat, but you …"

"I can be fat?"

"No, you're so skinny. You can eat whatever you want."

"How does your aunt know so much about what I like and dislike?"

"I guess it's because she's friends with your mother."

"You guess?" Gwen wondered about that.

"And she wants me to be happy."

"That's sweet of her." Gordon was almost endearing.

"So you want a hit of cocaine before we go to the Crab Shack? I've got a small stash here. I get it from some of the summer residents, especially the women."

Gwen didn't want to know any more. "No, I think I better get back home. I have to let my dog out." That dog might be a good idea after all. Maybe her mom had been right.

"Suit yourself. Just let me take a hit then we'll be on our way." Gordon raced the pontoon as much as you could race a pontoon then crashed into the dock at the Crab Shack.

"My uncle is not going to like this," he said as he surveyed the damage. Gwen took off her sandals and hopped from the pontoon into the shallow water. She pulled up her dress and waded to shore. Once on shore she slipped on her sandals and slunk away amidst the crowd that had gathered to see what had happened. She wanted to get away before the police – more precisely, Officer Kelley – showed up.

Having spent more time with Sam, he allowed her in with only a growl until she fed him and took him outside to do his duty.

"Sam, you have no idea the night I've had," she said as she scratched his jowls. He shook his head throwing spittle about him.

"Yep. That's the kind of night it was."

Chapter 14

No way Gwen was going out with Leon, not after Roger and Gordon. But then Leon came to church that morning and he gave her his puppy dog eyes. How could she let him down?

"I've got a surprise for you," he said when he picked her up. Somehow he had talked her into letting him drive her.

"Oh good," Gwen said with dread as she climbed in. "What's the surprise?"

"We're going dancing."

Why is it that short guys always want to dance? "Not the Crab Shack?"

"No. Better. Square dancing. I belong to a square dance club. You're going to love it. There's a buffet with great food and lessons for beginners before the regular dance starts."

"Leon, this is really your idea of a good time?"

"Don't knock it till you try it. Besides, it's a good way to meet girls, though most of them are my grandmother's age. But tonight, I won't have to worry about a partner because I'll have the prettiest girl there."

Leon was right about meeting people. Four men her grandfather's age hit on her while Leon was getting her a drink.

"Lemonade – the hard stuff."

"Oh boy." But, when the dancing started, it was actually fun, especially if you ignored the men who made a grab for her hand, missed and grabbed another body part during the allemande left.

Over all it wasn't a bad night. Especially in comparison to the last two nights.

"Thank you, Leon. That was almost fun," she said when he dropped her off. He walked her to her door.

"We meet every month. You want to come again?"

"I said almost."

"Then how about another date? Next time you choose what we do."

"I don't know, Leon. You aren't exactly my type."

"You mean that I'm not your type because I'm short."

"Well …"

"Who'd have thought you'd be a heightist."

"A heightist?"

"Yes, someone who judges people based on their height. And you being a minister."

"I'm not a heightist."

"Prove it. Go out with me again."

"Okay, all right. I'll go out with you, just no more square dancing." Gwen stepped on the first step of her porch, out of reach in case Leon wanted to try to kiss her. Sam growled from inside. "Time to go." Gwen ran up the rest of the stairs and into her home. From the door she could see Leon doing his celebratory "yes!" again. Then he square danced to his car.

What had she agreed to?

Chapter 15

"Okay, ladies. Time for a progress report. So far Gwen has gone out on three dates and only one is still in the running, the auto mechanic."

"Engine specialist," Margie corrected her.

"Whatever. You have to step up your game here. This is my daughter you're talking about." Laura turned to Hattie. "Hattie, what were you thinking? He was abducted by aliens?"

"Roger must have really liked Gwen to tell her that on the first date. Usually he waits till the third date."

"What were you thinking?"

"He's quirky. Who doesn't like quirky?"

"He's certifiable, and I ought to know."

"Roger's an acquired taste."

"And he stiffed Gwen for the bill for dinner. Who does that?"

"He feels really bad about that. He told me so. He was caught between pay checks."

"And what does he do for a living? Or does the mothership electronically send him money through the chip in his head?"

"He's a computer specialist."

"Yeah, at Best Buy," Bernice joined in.

"Your guy wasn't much better. He lives on a boat and works on his tan?"

"Not everyone can afford a boat."

"It's not his boat. It's his uncle's. And it's a pontoon. Who lives on a pontoon?"

"He has to save money for his head shots. He's a male model, you know. Do you know how hard it is to make it as a model? Likely he'll never make it, will end up living in a shack somewhere, but at least he's out there trying."

"And he snorts coke."

"I got to give you that. He crashed his uncle's boat."

"What about your guy?" Hattie asked Laura.

"He didn't show." Laura shrugged to dismiss the question.

"At least our guys showed up," Bernice said.

"My Leon is still in the running," Margie stated.

"Look, back to the plan. One man a month," Laura said.

"You have any idea how hard it is to find an eligible man who isn't flawed in some major way? All the good ones are already taken. Like I told you, this will never work," Bernice said.

"Hey, Leon's a good one," Margie said.

"That's why Gwen needs our help. Are you going to do this or not?" Laura ignored the comment.

"Okay," Hattie and Bernice agreed.

"Now get out there and find someone for my daughter."

"What about you?" Bernice asked. "What are you doing? Or do you realize how hopeless this is?"

"I'm working on it. You'll see." Laura smiled and poured herself more wine.

Chapter 16

Gwen pushed the classroom door open, her arms loaded with books and notes. She was prepared for this Bible Study. She was going to impress them with her knowledge. She had commentaries on Luke, commentaries on the three synoptic gospels – Matthew, Mark and Luke – she even knew what synoptic meant (ones that gave a synopsis of Jesus' life). She had a book of parallel constructions showing how the three gospels correlated. She had books on the early church community. And she had all of her notes. She almost dropped all of them when she heard a familiar voice.

"Here, let me help you with that." Leon. What was he doing here?

"No, let me help." Gordon, not him too? Does that mean …? She sighed. There was Roger, sitting in the front row of class, flashing his teeth as Leon and Gordon fought over her books and spilled them on the floor.

What next? Gwen rescued her notes from their all-too-eager grasp. "Thank you." She dismissed them and set out the books on her desk as proof of her expertise.

They sat down in the front row next to Roger where Leon made moon eyes at her. Roger sat back in his seat, a toothpick between his teeth. Gordon clasped a pen in his hand, waiting with open notebook to write down her words.

Gwen sighed and looked about the room. There were ten students total, a respectable number, six women, four men including her trio. Gwen had inherited this young adult Bible Study from the previous intern, along with the singles' ministry.

"You're a young adult and single," Pastor Joe had told her. He had a keen grasp of the obvious.

"Let's start by putting our desks in a semi-circle," Gwen instructed the class. Gordon almost tipped over his desk in his haste to get up and move his desk and move the other desks. Roger and Leon weren't far behind him.

"Isn't this better?" Gwen stood in the front center of the semi-circle, close to the desk with her resources. "My understanding is that you've been working your way through Luke."

"Yes," one of the six women stated. Her Bible was open as she prepared to start reading. "We are at the Sermon on the Plain, Luke chapter 6."

"Before we get started, let's take a moment to get to know each other. You have me at a disadvantage. You know who I am, but I don't know all of you. Introduce yourself and tell me why you are here." Gwen sat down at her desk so she could jot down names as each spoke.

"You know me," Roger winked at her.

"And me," Leon added.

"Yes, but the rest of the class may not know you. Let them know why you are here."

"Because I've got a crush on the teacher," Leon said.

"That's enough." Gwen stood up to end the conversation.

"But you didn't let me say why I'm here," Gordon said.

"That's okay. I'm sure it will be obvious."

"No, really. I'm here because I'm a fisherman. I live on a boat. Jesus knows about fishermen."

"He does. Thank you, Gordon," Gwen said.

"And the teacher has a rocking hard body," he added.

"Enough," Gwen said as the class giggled, followed by an awkward silence. She stood in front of the desk. "I know you are used to a traditional Bible Study, but I'd like to try something different. If you don't like it, we can always go back to the format you are used to."

"How different?" the young woman with the open Bible asked.

"I'm talking about acting out the readings," Gwen answered.

"We're adults, not the youth group. Isn't that what you do with teenagers?" the woman sitting next to the first asked.

"Why should they have all the fun?" Gwen looked about the room. No one showed any interest but her trio. "Just give it a try. Who's game?"

"I am," Leon jumped up followed by Gordon.

"There, we have two volunteers. First, we need to set the scene. Jesus is being followed by hordes of people. He sets them down on a plain at the foot of the mountain and begins to preach." Gwen opened up her Bible. "Luke's Gospel is considered the gospel for the poor. You know that, right?" Gwen looked around the room to get an idea how much they already knew. "Luke has the shepherds, the poorest of the poor, being the first to visit baby Jesus. He shows concern for the poor and needy repeatedly. He also mentions women more than the other gospels. His gospel is good news to the poor. We see that in the beginning of the Sermon on the Plain, Luke's beatitudes. There's Jesus, giving comfort to the poor." Gwen walked into the middle of the semi-circle and began to read, addressing one side of the class. She read with compassion in her voice.

"Blessed are you who are poor, for the kingdom of God is yours.

"Blessed are you who are now hungry, for you will be satisfied.

"Blessed are you who are now weeping, for you will laugh.

"Blessed are you when people hate you and when they exclude and insult you, and denounce your name as evil on account of the Son of Man. Rejoice and leap for joy on that day! Behold, your reward will be great in heaven. For their ancestors treated the prophets in the same way."

Then she swung over to the other side of the class, pointing her finger at them as her voice grew louder and condemning.

"But woe to you who are rich, for you have received your consolation.

"But woe to you who are filled now, for you will be hungry.

"Woe to you who laugh now, for you will grieve and weep.

"Woe to you when all speak well of you, for their ancestors treated the false prophets in this way."

Gwen closed her Bible and addressed the class.

"Do you see what Jesus is doing here? He's comforting the poor and afflicting the rich and comfortable. His message is one of good news to the poor and lowly, not so good to the rich and powerful. Is it any wonder they had him killed? We have to get to know Jesus again, as if for the first time. Forget about all you've been told. We need to know the real Jesus, not the baby in the manger or the resurrected, ephemeral Jesus, but Jesus the man, an itinerant preacher with no place to lay his head. A man on fire with the love of God. A man loved by the masses of the poor, hated by the religious leaders. A revolutionary."

She stopped and motioned to Leon and Gordon. "Leon and Gordon, come over here."

She opened her Bible. "I want you to act out the passages I read," she said and started to read. *"But to you who hear I say, love your enemies, do good to those who hate you, bless those who curse you, pray for those who mistreat you. To the person who strikes you on one cheek, offer the other one as well."* She stopped and nodded at Leon and Gordon. Leon cowered as Gordon raised his hand to strike.

"No, that's not what Jesus meant. Leon, stand up." Gwen raised her hand as if to slap him. Her hand grazed his face, pushing it to one side. "Now offer the other," she told Leon. He turned his cheek back toward Gwen so the only way she could hit him was with her back hand. "Do you see? This is not an act of fear. It's an act of rebellion, defiance. What slave would stand up to his master like this? It's an act of strength. This is not the action of a subordinate, but the action of an equal. It's also an act of love. I love you too much to allow you to demean yourself, brutalize yourself. I love you enough to stand up to you. This is the core of the non-violent gospel. It's not for wimps. Jesus is telling the poor to stand up to their tormentors, show them they have no real power over them. Their master can't make them cower in fear before them. Let's go on."

She started to read again, *"And from the person who takes your cloak, do not withhold even your tunic."* She turned to Leon and Gordon. "Act this out."

Leon pretended to give Gordon his cloak then the shirt off his back, then covered himself as if naked.

"What are you doing?" Gwen asked over the laughter of the class.

"Well, if I gave him both my cloak and my tunic, wouldn't I be down to my underwear?"

"You would. Does anyone remember a famous saint who did just that?" When no one responded, Gwen replied, "Francis of Assisi. When Francis' father demanded he return the goods he had given away to the poor, Francis stripped naked in front of the whole crowd and walked away. Must have been quite a scene. Nakedness was not allowed in Jesus' time, but the shame fell more on the person who observed the nakedness or caused it rather than the naked person. Thus, the person giving his cloak and tunic brought shame to the one asking for it. Another way for the poor to stand up to creditors demanding what little they had. Let's try another one: How would you act out this passage – *"He told them a parable, can a blind person guide a blind person?"*

Both men closed their eyes, stretched out their hands and bumped into each other. Gordon tried to lead Leon, bumping into desks as the class laughed.

"Do you think Jesus had the crowds laughing at this?" one of the class asked.

"Maybe. I do know Jesus was a great, compelling speaker to have so many people following him, hanging onto his every word. Thank you, Leon and Gordon. Let's give them a hand," Gwen began a round of clapping. Leon and Gordon bowed and went back to their seats. "Do you think you could do something like this on Sunday?"

"What are you talking about?" The woman with the open Bible asked.

"Act out the readings. Put on skits to entertain, plus make a point. I want to get a drama team together for the church. I thought this group might be interested."

"I don't know. I came here to study the Bible, not play act," she said, looking over at the woman sitting next to her for affirmation.

"Isn't that what we just did? Studied the Bible?"

"Maybe."

"Let's take a break. We can talk about it later." The students went to the table at the side of the room where cookies, lemonade and coffee were provided. Gwen heard a slow clapping coming from the door of the classroom.

"Officer Kelley? How long have you been here?"

"Long enough," he said with a smile.

"What can I do for you?"

"Rather, it's what I can do for you. Seems your dog got loose, was terrorizing the neighborhood cats."

"But Sam wouldn't do that. He wouldn't hurt anyone."

"You tell that to the cats."

"How did he get out? Where is he?"

"He's in the squad car. I recognized the description so I took the call."

"I'm so sorry."

"I'm not. I enjoyed your class. You really believe all that non-violence nonsense?"

"Of course, or I wouldn't be teaching it."

"You try turning the other cheek in a gun fight. You wouldn't live to tell about it."

"Jesus wasn't referring to guns."

"They had bows and arrows and spears in his time."

"That wasn't the example, was it?" Gwen pushed past him to get to the parking lot.

"I'm just saying, non-violence doesn't work if you are dealing with a psychopath."

"Are you done? Because if you are, I'd like to get my dog." The ripple of pleasure she had experienced when she first saw the officer had given way to annoyance. What did he know about non-violence anyway?

As if he had read her mind, he stated. "You know, we do learn about ways to handle potentially violent situations. How to keep a situation from escalating, diffuse explosive states. It's part of our training."

"And I know about Jesus and his message of non-violent love. It's part of my training," Gwen stated while Officer Kelley let Sam out of the back seat of the squad car.

"Maybe you can tell me more about it sometime."

"Sure. Whenever," Gwen snapped as she dragged Sam to the rectory.

"Great. I'll hold you to it," Officer Kelley said as she walked away.

"Naughty dog." Gwen brought him into the kitchen, checked to make sure he had water, then made sure the door was locked securely behind her before going back to the church center.

How had he gotten out?

Chapter 17

The singles group met at a different restaurant on the third Wednesday of each month.

"Everybody has to eat and no one wants to eat out alone," explained Sheila, the woman who had started the group. All Gwen had to do was show up. Easy peasey. She wasn't surprised when her trio of beaus showed up as well. She was beginning to expect them. They had even started attending Sunday services, sitting close to the front where they could wave at her on the Sundays she preached. It was one way to get butts in the pew.

All three had gotten to know some of the other members of the group through the Bible study since there was overlap in attendance. When she had come back to the Bible study after rescuing Sam from the squad car, they had been chatting with the other members. Part of her had wanted to warn the women, the other part was relieved to have their attention diverted elsewhere. Today they were busy chatting with the ladies. They hardly stopped to acknowledge her presence when she sat down. She smiled in relief, then looked through the menu. When she looked up, she saw Officer Kelley in civilian clothes with the blond she had seen him with that first night. He nodded in her direction. She blocked her face with her menu as he walked over to the table.

"You been talking any more about non-violence?"

Gwen pulled her head out from behind her menu. "I have."

"Remember, you promised me you would tell me more about it."

"I didn't promise anything," Gwen started to say but was cut short as Officer Kelley greeted others at the table.

"Leon, right? And Roger, and Gordon?" He shook their hands and talked to others at the table before leaving.

"Remember," he said to her with a tip of his hand.

"You know Officer Kelley?" the woman next to her asked.

"Apparently me and everyone else."

"He's so cute."

"If you like that type."

"Strong and handsome, yeah."

Gwen went back to examining her menu. At this rate she would have it memorized, except the words refused to remain in her brain.

"You memorizing that menu?" Another male voice.

"And if I am, what's that to you?" Gwen lowered her menu expecting Officer Kelley had returned.

"Nothing, except it's hiding your pretty face."

"Do I know you?" Gwen looked the man over. Medium height, brown hair, appears to be in his thirties.

"No, but I would like to get to know you."

Gwen looked to either side of her. "Me? You talking to me?"

"No one else. Would you mind if I called you sometime? You're Gwen, right? From St. Luke's?"

"Sure, I guess. And you're?"

"Wayne."

"Okay, Wayne. Call me." Gwen dismissed him without giving him her number. She somehow knew he didn't need it.

"Ooooh, you're a man magnet," the woman next to her said. "I'm Charlotte."

"No man magnet. That's not me at all." But then, that was how she had met Leon, Roger and Gordon. The dates had been disasters, but she looked at the three happily talking to other women at the table. The results weren't that bad. They had even helped her at the Bible Study. Still, she wondered where these men were coming from.

"How about we go out together some time? I could be your wing man, or woman," Charlotte said.

"I'll think about it." She didn't have a lot of time for dating, not with all of her church responsibilities. Besides why start dating someone when she would be gone after a year? Gwen hid behind her menu and thought about her latest conversation with Marcie as the group about her chatted.

"Because it's a year, duh," Marcie had said. "Do you really want to go for a year without a date? You're beginning to sound like a minister already."

"But I'll be going back to Chicago."

"So, Chicago's not exactly the end of the world. Have some fun. What would it hurt for you to go out with a couple of different guys?"

"I don't know. Something's not quite right about all of this."

"You worry too much. Enjoy yourself." Maybe Marcie was right. She did worry too much. And she did like having fun. She enjoyed going out with her friends from seminary, but this was different. Now she had a role to maintain, a position at the church. How was she to fill that position and the expectations that come with it and still have a private life, a social life?

She met weekly with Pastor Joe to discuss how everything was going, ask questions, get insights. He had also arranged for her to meet with a spiritual director for guidance on her spiritual life.

"Isn't that what you are for?" Gwen had asked when Pastor Joe had given her the name.

"I'm your boss and mentor. We may talk about spiritual matters, but you need someone else to talk to. Someone removed from your position here that you can talk to about what is happening between you and God."

Gwen had plenty of advisors at seminary. She didn't see the need to meet with yet another person. Still, she had met with one of her professors at college. That was how she had ended up at seminary. She guessed it wouldn't hurt too much, and maybe would help. Gwen had started out at seminary in a general ministry program. She had pre-requisites to fill and wasn't sure what she wanted to do with her life after graduation. Maybe the missions. Maybe Religious Education. Maybe some other ministry position. She hadn't transferred into preparation for ordained ministry till after her first year. She still wasn't sure this was what she wanted to do with her life. She figured that was part of what this internship was about. She had one more year till ordination after she completed the internship.

She had also been taking Improv classes with Second City in Chicago and had completed their course. It had been fun, but not enough. She wanted something more. She still wasn't sure what that was, but ordained ministry was an option. Her dad had been great about supporting her through her searching, helping with tuition and other expenses, even when it didn't look like he was getting much of a return on his money, even when she extended the four-year program to five. She wasn't going to be the eternal student though. Eventually she would have to find a paid position, not just a job, but a vocation. Something she could commit her life to. She had found a set of beliefs in the Lutheran Church. Something she could believe in. Something she could remain faithful to for the rest of her life. And she had found someone to believe in — Jesus. Now, if she could find someone to spend the rest of her life with, that would be it. Her life's direction would be set. But not too fast, and not now. She didn't want to rush. She wanted someone, and she didn't.

Time enough to make those mistakes once she was ordained. For now, she needed to focus on getting through this internship. And for tonight, she had to make the best of this dinner. She sighed then smiled as she placed her order.

Chapter 18

Gwen peeked into the hospital room, announcing her presence with a hesitant knock on the partially open door. She didn't know why Pastor Joe insisted on her visiting this woman, but then why did he ask her to do any of the many things he did? She supposed they were to be "learning experiences."

A woman in her thirties was saying goodbye to her husband. She wore a big smile that lightened her face despite the bandages covering her head. She grabbed his face, squeezed his cheeks, then kissed him again, before letting go.

"Okay, now get out of here."

Gwen thought she saw tears in his eyes as he prepared to leave.

"I'm sorry. I can come back later," Gwen said.

"No reason to be sorry. Terry was just leaving. You have perfect timing." The young woman smiled that infectious smile at her. The man slipped out the door without acknowledging her presence.

"You're the new intern at St. Luke's, Gwen," the woman stated. "Pastor Joe told me you would be coming."

"And you're Elizabeth."

"Liz." She pointed at a chair next to the hospital bed. "What can I do for you?"

Gwen laughed. "It seems Pastor Joe thought there was something I could do for you."

"Oh, no, that's not the case. Tell me about yourself."

"Not much to tell. Sounds like Pastor Joe already told you enough."

"He just told me the uninteresting stuff. That you are the intern and you grew up in Cascade Falls. I believe I know your parents, Dr. Thompson and Laura, the church secretary."

"You already know so much about me. Tell me about you."

"It's so boring. I'm recovering from brain surgery. My third one. I have a slow growing tumor. It's not cancerous, so life is good, right? I just have to have surgery now and then."

Gwen sat in silence as she pondered what she had been told. What could she say? "Tell me about your family," she finally said. The words sounded even more feeble now that she had said them than they had in her head, but they did the trick.

"You met Terry, my husband. He's a plumber, works for Reese's Plumbing. Perhaps you know the family?"

"Who doesn't? Mrs. Reese teaches sixth grade."

"That's my husband's boss' wife. His sister is married to Pastor Joe."

Gwen smiled and nodded her head. Of course she knew the infamous Kathleen. Everyone knew Kathleen. "Do you have any children?"

"Yes, my son TJ – Terrence Junior, and my daughter, Leia. I call her princess." Liz pulled out pictures from the drawer of the table that slid over the bed. "TJ's nine and Leia's six."

"I've seen them at church."

"They are hard to miss. Leia is a spit-fire, so full of spunk. TJ's more laid back, like his dad."

"And Leia's like you."

"Some say so."

"So, the prognosis, it's good?" Gwen decided to bring the conversation back to Liz's surgery.

"As good as it gets with brain tumors. You know, one time they put me in the psych ward. Thought I was crazy when it was just the tumor. I kept telling everyone I wasn't crazy, but then that's what everyone in the psych ward says, so no one believed me. That's where I met Pastor Joe. He believed me. He helped Terry get the job at Reese's Plumbing. That was five years ago, after Leia was born. After that, we joined the church."

"Must have been hard, being in the hospital with a baby at home and a toddler."

"Psych ward. The psych ward. It was, but that's in the past. I live for the future."

"What is that future?"

"Hopefully no more surgeries. The surgeon says because of where the tumor is, he can't remove all of it. It keeps coming back. I just want to watch my children grow up. There was a time, though. Don't call me crazy if I tell you."

Gwen nodded her encouragement for Liz to continue.

"It was after my second surgery. The anesthetic wore off. I was in extreme pain, but no one would listen to me. Then, just when I didn't think I could stand it anymore, I was lifted off of the bed by these loving arms and the pain went away. Then I was lowered back down until the pain got bad again. Again, the arms lifted me. There was a peace I can't explain, but it was real." Tears welled in her eyes as she remembered. Gwen reached over and placed her hand on Liz's hand.

"Some people tried to tell me I was just imagining it. That it was just my mind's way of shutting down in the face of extreme pain, protecting me. That's what those psychologists from the psych ward tried to tell me, but I know they are wrong. It was real, as real as you sitting here. I was lifted up by God's hands. Only Pastor Joe listened." She pulled out two prayer cards. On one was the picture of a baby held in the palm of a hand and the passage from Isaiah, *"I will never forget you my people, I hold you in the palm of my hand."* On the other was the picture of an eagle flying amidst clouds and the words adapted from Exodus 19 verse 4, *"I will bear you on eagle's wings and bring you home to me."*

"He gave me these prayer cards. I had been raised Baptist, but stopped attending church in high school. I had forgotten so many of the Scripture quotes I had memorized as a child. And now, from the surgeries and the meds, my head is too foggy to remember, but I hold onto these cards. They remind me of that peace I experienced."

As if on cue, Liz shut her eyes. The vibrancy and smile faded from her face, replaced by the peace of near sleep. Liz opened her eyes as Gwen stood up.

"I'm sorry if I tired you out," Gwen stated.

"I tire easily. Come again." Liz smiled and extended her hand. Gwen gave her hand a slight squeeze then placed it back on the hospital bed. The pale hand laid in contrast against the white, antiseptic sheet. Liz closed her eyes. This time she didn't wake up as Gwen walked out the door.

"How was Liz Schultz when you visited?" Pastor Joe asked as she walked into their weekly meeting.

"Good. Smiling. Peaceful." Gwen sat down in her accustomed seat.

"Did she tell you about the prognosis?"

"Not much. Just that she had a slow growing tumor and the surgeon couldn't remove all of it."

"Yes. But they aren't able to do any more surgeries."

"She didn't tell me that. She seemed to be under the impression that they'll keep doing surgeries. Did the doctor tell her?"

"Yes, but how much she was able to take in, I don't know. She may be in denial."

"What will happen next? I thought she was going home."

"She is going home. This last surgery bought her some time. We don't know how long she has until the tumor grows back. Until then, she will be able to stay with her family, enjoy the time she has."

"Are we talking months? Years?"

"Don't know. How much time do I have? Patients always ask that question. Doctors don't like to give an answer. They don't like being wrong. How much time do any of us have? Years? Months? Decades? We don't know the hour. We do know it's coming for all of us."

At twenty-six, thoughts of death were not on her radar. Why was Pastor Joe putting her in such positions? Why can't she just focus on the young adults, and maybe the seniors, homebound church members? Yes, they were dying, but they were old. It was fitting. This woman, Liz, wasn't that much older than she was.

"Care for the dying, comfort for grieving families, they're very important parts of church ministry. Your congregation will forgive you many faults as long as you care for them at their time of loss. They also may never forgive you if you don't. Remember that."

"But why someone so young?"

"Only God knows. Last year we had two young people die from opioid overdoses. Yes, the opioid problem is present, even here in Cascade Falls. We are not immune to any of the ills of the society we live in. As ministers, we need to know how to be with our people during their struggles and their losses."

Gwen was still thinking about Liz and what Pastor Joe had said when she returned to her office. She was brought out of her ruminations when the phone rang.

"There's a Wayne on line one for you," her mom's voice broke into her thoughts.

"Who?"

"Wayne. Says you're expecting his call."

"Oh, yeah. Wayne." The man from dinner the other night. She had forgotten about him. "Put him through." He could be a nice break from thoughts of death and dying.

"Gwen, about that date. The one you promised the other night."

"I didn't promise," Gwen started to say then thought better of it. "Yes."

"Saturday night. The Italian restaurant downtown."

After the fiasco at Giglio with Roger last month, Gwen had been avoiding the place. "How about some other place?"

"Okay. The Steakhouse. Mom likes that place too."

"What?" What was he saying about his mother?

"Seven o'clock. You want me to pick you up?"

"No, I'll meet you there." He must have meant his mother had recommended the place. A date might be just what she needed.

Chapter 19

The Steakhouse was smoky and dim when Gwen arrived a little after seven. She didn't want to get there before Wayne and have to sit alone at a table till he came. No need to worry. Wayne saw her and waved to her before she had a chance to ask the maître 'de. It looked like someone was with him. Maybe they were just keeping him company till she arrived?

Wayne stood up and pulled out her chair for her so she could sit down. Sitting next to Wayne was an older woman, fiftyish, she figured.

"Mom, this is Gwen, the girl I was telling you about. Gwen this is my mom."

Gwen forced her mouth back from where it felt like it had fallen out of her jaw. "Pleased to meet you, Mrs. …" she managed to say before being interrupted.

"Just call me Martha. No need for formalities. Wayne has already told me so much about you. I feel I know you."

"You realize this is our first date, don't you?"

"Oh, that. Of course. Wayne always invites me to his first dates. How else would he know it was worth pursuing a second date without me along?" Martha smiled and placed her linen napkin in her lap. "He told me you work for St. Luke's church. That could be a problem. We're Pentecostal. Aren't Lutherans close to being Catholic? All those rites and ritual prayers. And isn't St. Luke's ELCA? That's the liberal branch of the Lutheran Church."

"Mom," Wayne stopped her. "I thought we agreed we wouldn't bring this up right away."

"Who agreed? I didn't agree to anything. Now I'm sure Gwen is a lovely girl, but I have to know where she stands on this matter or we might as well go home." Martha looked back at Gwen. "So, tell me, Gwen, would any children you and Wayne have be raised Lutheran or Pentecostal."

"I think I need to leave." Gwen started to stand up.

"No, wait. You can't leave yet. We haven't even had appetizers. You can't leave before appetizers," Wayne insisted.

"No, I think I can." Gwen stood up. "Thank you for … hell, thanks for nothing, Wayne. You and your mother enjoy your dinner."

"I'll call you," Wayne called after her.

"She swore, in front of your mother. A good Pentecostal girl wouldn't do that," Gwen heard as she walked out.

She would have laughed, but she was so hungry. What would she do now? She hated eating by herself in restaurants. She decided to go to Burger Barn and pick up a meal to go.

She was surprised to see Leon and Gordon on what appeared to be a double date. She placed her order then went to their table.

"Gwen," Leon said, "so nice to see you. Do you want to join us?" Gwen recognized the two women from the singles group.

"No, thank you. I don't mean to interrupt your date. I just wanted to say hi."

"No interruption," Leon said. "We'd be happy to have you join us." One look at their dates and Gwen knew that wasn't true.

"No, you enjoy your date. I've got work to do for tomorrow's service. I'm just going to take my burger home to eat."

Gwen went back to the counter to pick up her take-out. Leon excused himself and followed her.

"You know, we aren't exclusive," Leon said.

"We?" Gwen said using finger quotations. "We are not 'we.' We aren't anything. One date, Leon. It was only one date."

"Yes, but you said you would go out with me again. That's more than you did with Roger and Gordon."

"Maybe because you refused to give up."

"Some say that's my most endearing quality."

Gwen picked up her bag of fries and greasy burger.

"Just say the word and I'll dump her," Leon whispered.

"No, Leon. Go back to your date."

"Well, don't say I didn't give you a chance," Leon walked back to his table.

Once outside, Gwen stopped briefly to look into the restaurant window. She saw Leon back at his table. The woman he was with was laughing at something he said. They looked like they were having fun. She wondered if maybe she had been too quick to turn down the invitation. It would have been much more pleasant to sit in a restaurant, eating with friends, than going home alone.

"Looking for someone?"

Gwen jumped at the familiar male voice. Officer Kelley again. "Don't tell me Sam's escaped again."

"No, I'm just getting something to eat. Care to join me?"

"No, I'm sorry. I can't. I got mine to go." How could she go back inside and eat with this police officer after she had just blown off Leon and the rest?

"Then I'll get mine to go too. Better that way. If I get a call while I'm eating, I'll already have a bag so I can eat it later."

"All right. I'll wait out here" Officer Kelley gave her a puzzled look then went inside. Gwen moved to where she couldn't be seen by any of the group of four.

"Lurking in the shadows?" Liam said when he came out with his take-out bag. "I could arrest you on suspicion of preparing to commit a crime."

"And what crime would that be?"

"Preparing to break someone's heart. Wasn't that Leon and Gordon in there?"

"Yes, and if you didn't notice, they are on dates."

"You aren't dating?"

"God, no," Gwen blurted out, then covered her mouth. Another unseemly response from a church minister. "I mean, gosh, no."

Liam smiled. "I know what you mean." They walked to a city park and sat on a bench.

"What about you? That blond you are dating. Would she approve of you sitting on a park bench with another woman?"

"She knows I have to put up with all kinds of characters in my line of work."

"So do I."

"Right. Ministry, police work. They do have that in common."

"Except I'm only armed with God's word."

"And how is that working for you?"

"Just fine. It's working just fine."

"As for me, I like to back up God's word with my Glock."

Gwen laughed, unwrapped her burger and took a bite. She watched as Officer Kelley took a big bite of his double bacon cheeseburger.

"Fries?" she offered

"No thanks. Got to stay in shape for chasing down criminals."

"You'll have to chase a lot of criminals to burn the calories from that burger."

"Or dogs. Chasing dogs." They ate in silence for a while.

"So, the blonde?" Gwen broke the silence.

"Complicated. Your trio?"

"Not complicated. They are just friends."

"Who want to be more than friends."

"I think they know my thoughts on that."

"Which are?" A mixture of mustard, relish and grease slipped out of his burger and onto his uniform.

Gwen pulled a napkin out of her bag. "Here, let me."

As she wiped his shirt, she could feel the hardness of his bullet proof vest, then looked up to see he was watching her. "There, all better." She tossed the napkin into her bag and stared straight forward into the night. Liam wiped his hands on a napkin, crinkled the napkin into his burger wrapper and placed it into his bag then reached for Gwen's bag and tossed both into a nearby trash can.

"Guess I better get back to work," Liam said.

"And I better get home and let Sam out."

"I'll walk you to your car."

"No need."

Gwen heard the radio blare. Liam answered the call. "A domestic. I've got to go."

Gwen watched his steady lope to the squad car. It hadn't been such a bad night after all. She sighed. If only he wasn't already taken.

Chapter 20

Dew sparkled on the grass as Gwen went for her morning run with Sam. Sam didn't always cooperate. Sometimes he stopped her mid-run or pulled her off the sidewalk in order to sniff a bush. Still, the company was nice. She stopped and waited for Sam to finish his morning constitutional, turning aside to give him privacy, when another jogger came by. Instead of passing her as expected, he slowed down and jogged in place.

"Mind if I join you? I've noticed you jogging each morning."

"As long as you don't mind a big dog stopping every few feet." Gwen figured, what could be the harm in this? No one would try anything with Sam along.

"Don't mind at all." He started to run alongside her. "You're Gwen, the new intern at St. Luke's, aren't you?"

"Do you attend St. Luke's?"

"No, but I might start."

"So how do you know my name?"

"I've asked around. Wasn't hard to find out. How many pretty girls are out at this hour of the morning running with a mastiff?"

"I guess not too many."

"You guessed right. I'm Evan." They jogged a few more blocks, both breathing too hard to carry on a conversation. "This is my turn,"

"Appears you know my routine."

"Would you like to go out some time?" Gwen looked him over. He didn't look scary. No ax murderer hiding in sweatpants. Why not? They agreed to meet for a game of tennis later that week.

"I'm not that good but I can still hold a mean racket," Gwen told him before heading home to take a shower and begin her day. It was off to a good start even if she had to meet with the spiritual director Pastor Joe had recommended. How hard could an hour a month talking about God be?

Adelle was in her back yard when Gwen arrived.

"Back here," she shouted when Gwen hit the doorbell. Strains of "Take Me Out to the Ball Game" sounded in the house as Gwen stepped through the gate to the back yard.

"So much to do this time of year. Weeds to pull. Bushes to trim. You don't mind, do you, dear?" Adelle clipped roses, placing them into a basket with her gloved hands. The odors of late summer exuberance filled the yard. Flowers, newly clipped, rose scents, the mustiness of decaying growth.

"I guess not." This wasn't what she had expected. When she had met with Mrs. Peregrine her senior year in college, they always sat in her office in seats designated for such conversations. She met with Pastor Joe in his office. The advisors and counsellors at school always had a set place for meeting with students. This was different. She swatted a bee away.

"He's not going to hurt you, you know. Honey bees don't sting unless you give them a good reason to. It's wasps you have to watch out for. Nasty creatures. They'll sting you for no reason. Just out of meanness. If you happen to be in their path or close to their nest, they'll sting you, then run away. Like some people. Honey bees, though ..." Adele stopped and smelled a flower, inhaling deeply before continuing. "We need them. I'm always happy to have them in my garden. The flowers are lusher and more splendiferous when there are more bees to cross pollinate them. Some in the neighborhood, they complained when the farmer down the road a ways starting keeping bees. They watch too many horror movies about killer bees. Not me. I like bees. I don't bother them. They don't bother me."

Gwen wondered what this had to do with spiritual direction but didn't ask. She was afraid she would get an answer.

"Pastor Joe tells me you're the new intern."

"And he tells me you're a former nun."

"That's right. I was a Dominican, a preaching order."

"Why did you leave?"

"I guess you could say God called me away from the convent."

"You guess? You don't know?"

"Do any of us really know with certainty what God wants of us? Except, of course, to be kind. He's pretty clear about that. The other stuff though. He leaves that to us to sort out."

"If you really believed that, how can you be a spiritual director?"

"Because most people need help sorting it out."

Gwen waved away a fly.

"I like being out here in my garden. God speaks to me here, in nature." Adelle clipped another rose.

"And what does God say?"

"It isn't necessarily what he says. It's what I hear."

Gwen could feel ripples of annoyance, drops sliding down her spine, like the beads of sweat forming on her brow and sliding down the bridge of her nose. What a waste of time.

"You look hot. Let's get some lemonade."

"That would be good." Gwen wiped her forehead with the back of her hand. She hoped they were going inside but Adelle instructed her to sit at a round table on her back deck. Gwen tried to find some shade to hide under from the overhead umbrella on the table. It was going to be another hot late August day. Adelle had left her garden gloves on the table where Gwen could see the green and brown stains from dirt and plants pulled. The basket of roses Adelle had taken inside. She came out with two frosted glasses of lemonade.

"Drink up. Lemons are good for your digestion."

"Thank you." Gwen gulped the mixture of icy sweet tartness down. It did taste good. She hadn't realized how thirsty she was.

Adelle watched her as she drank. Gwen stopped as she became all too aware of her penetrating gaze. "So, tell me. What is your deepest desire?"

Gwen put her glass down. "What?"

"Your deepest desire. What is it? God often speaks to us through our desires."

"Ah, I guess to do his will."

"No, that's too easy. Everyone says that. Tell me more about yourself. Your fears. Your desires."

Gwen paused. Did she dare tell this woman she had just met her fears and desires?

"You're living in the manse, aren't you?"

"Yes."

"How is that?"

"It's okay."

"Again, too easy. Tell me." Adelle was not accepting that as an answer.

"Okay. I don't like it."

"Why not?"

"Because … it's so big and lonely. I'd rather be in an apartment building with other people."

"Not your parents' home?"

"No, that would be worse than the manse."

"What's your greatest fear? If you can't tell me your desires, tell me your fears. They are often connected."

"How so?"

"You tell me. Tell me your greatest fear, and I'll tell you your greatest desire."

"Okay." Gwen looked across the yard as she thought. "I guess my greatest fear is that I will be alone. It's not that I can't handle living alone. I just don't want to live that way all my life."

"And yet you are living by yourself in a manse. And you are picking a lonely profession."

"How so? Ministry is all about people, being with people, helping them, helping them in their relationship with God."

"Yes, and it's a lonely place to be, always helping others. Where do you find your help?"

"From God."

Adelle broke out in laughter. "Too easy. You keep looking for the easy answers. The arrogance and zeal of youth. So sure you don't need anything or anyone but God."

"But," Gwen paused and frowned. "Isn't that what Paul tells us? God's grace is enough for us?"

"Paul was very driven."

"You're saying Paul was wrong?"

"I'm saying, Paul was Paul. You need to be Gwen. If God is enough for us, then why do we need each other? God knows our needs. That's why God sends people into our lives."

Gwen frowned again. "I told you my fear. What is my desire?"

"To be connected. Not just surface relationships but to have deep relationships."

Gwen felt a surge of tears form at the words. Tears she was determined to fight. "Maybe so."

"But you're also afraid of your need for connection. That's why you are looking for something safe and secure to be connected to, a set of beliefs to give meaning to your life. That's why you chose ministry. That's why you chose God. You are looking for something safe to believe, someone safe you can trust. If you can't trust God, who can you trust?"

"You tell me. You're the spiritual director."

"I prefer guide. I'm just a guide along the way. You need to find your own way. I'll help you avoid the pitfalls."

"You're saying, God didn't call me into ministry? I called myself?"

"I didn't say anything of the kind. God knows our fears and desires. He uses them to call us to him. But if you are looking for safety, you've chosen the wrong path."

"What are you talking about?"

"Being a minister is like being a gardener. You are working in the Lord's garden. It's good work, but it's hard work. It will transform you. Look around. Look at all the vines and wild flowers overtaking the garden." Adelle led her off of the porch, back to the garden. Gwen gazed upon the wild abundance. Adelle waited.

"It's beautiful," Gwen said.

Adelle reached over and started clipping and pulling flowers with seeming abandon.

"What are you doing?" Gwen asked. "Why are you destroying such beauty?"

"Because sometimes in life, flowers are struck down in their prime. Sometimes, that which we have labored long to build, is torn down in a moment. Sometimes the good is destroyed along with the weeds. And we don't know why. If you want to be in ministry, be prepared to be pruned." She reached up and clipped a branch from a grape vine.

"I think that's enough for today," Adelle said as she went back to her gardening, pulling weeds with no further word of dismissal.

Gwen stood there, preparing to say something. The words wouldn't form in her mouth. She let herself out.

"That woman you sent me to …" Gwen said to Pastor Joe later that day.

"Adelle. How did it go?"

"It didn't. She's crazy. Kept talking about her garden."

"Did you learn anything?"

"No."

"Then keep going back until you do," was all he said.

Gwen shook her head in disbelief. What a waste of time.

Chapter 21

Evan was warming up, hitting balls against the backboard when she got to the tennis courts. He was good. She squirmed as she watched him slam balls. She had been athletic in high school but softball had been her sport. She had never quite mastered tennis. But she was okay. She figured she could hold her own in a friendly competition.

She went up alongside him and started to hit balls against the backboard as well.

"You're good," she told him.

"It's a good way to blow off steam." Evan smashed a ball against the board.

"Bad day?" Gwen lightly hit the ball against the board.

"Just a day like any other day since Patrice left."

"Patrice?

"My old girlfriend. She left me."

"That must hurt."

"Yeah, well, that's life. Ready to play?"

"Sure." But are you ready, Gwen thought. "You and Patrice, you ever play tennis?"

"Only every day."

"She was good then?"

"The best."

"When did you say you broke up?"

"I didn't say. A few weeks ago."

They took their respective places. "I'm not as good as Patrice. I'm pretty rusty. I hope you'll take it easy on me."

Evan lobbed one over the net. She easily returned it for a point. "Just letting you warm up," Evan said.

They lobbed balls back and forth. Love-love – tie score. Gwen was starting to get the feel for the game again.

"Love, that's right. That's what Patrice said. She said she loved me. Right." He slammed one at Gwen. "Game point. You serve."

Gwen served. Evan easily returned it, again smashing it right at her so Gwen had to jump back to avoid being hit. "Hey, I thought you were going to take it easy on me?"

"Like Patrice took it easy on me? She broke my heart."

He returned Gwen's serve with a hard hit coming at her. Gwen hit the next two serves into the net.

"Game, set, match. You win."

"Don't patronize me. I know you threw the game. I hate being patronized. Patrice was so patronizing." He pulled balls out of the bag and started hitting them at her.

"Hey, I'm not Patrice. I'm not the one who broke your heart," Gwen yelled between dodging tennis balls.

"That's right." Evan stopped in mid-swing. "I don't know what got into me."

"You want to talk about it?"

"What's there to talk about? … I'm sorry. You want to try again?"

"No, I think I've had enough tennis."

"At least let me make it up to you with dinner."

"No, I think I better head home. I need to shower, then take Sam out."

"The same excuse Patrice always had." Gwen could see the rage growing again. She hurried to her car amidst more tennis balls expertly aimed at her head.

She decided to vary her running routine after that. Were there any sane men in Cascade Falls?

Chapter 22

The sun sparkled off the waterfall and the streams of water that made up the miniature golf course at Cascade Hills park. The youth group was having its end-of-summer, welcome-fall picnic at the park which featured a miniature golf course, go-karts, picnic area, tennis courts and play ground. Dale and Ava were in charge of the food. Simple fare. Grilled hot dogs and bratwursts, chips, salad for the more health-conscious, watermelon, pop and bottled water. The teens had set out in groups of four to play miniature golf. Gwen was bringing up the rear with the last group which included Grace, Josie and Trevor. Gwen helped Josie manage the steps and winding paths, letting other groups play through when they took too long at a hole.

"Can I join another group?" Trevor complained as it took Josie and Grace an average of six shots each hole.

"Sure, go ahead." Gwen sent him on his way to the next group.

Gwen had been quite the miniature golfer in her time. Now she preferred real golf, but still had a few trick shots. She remembered how to navigate the bumps and turns of this course to come in under par each time. She quietly rejoiced at each hole-in-one, preferring to cheer on Grace and Josie. From behind them, she noticed a man watching her.

"Did you want to play through?" Gwen asked.

"I'm in no hurry," he stated while the other two members of this threesome welcomed the offer. "How about I play with you?" He waved the couple on and joined Gwen. "You look like you are having more fun anyway."

"Really?"

"Sure. I see how you play. You know your way around this course. I don't think it has taken you more than two strokes to complete any of the holes so far."

"You don't mind waiting for us?" Grace asked.

"Maybe I can give you some tips," he suggested. "I'm Ian."

"Gwen, and this is Grace and Josie."

"Pleased to meet you." Ian entertained Grace and Josie with his trick shots then helped them with their turns, freeing Gwen to shift her focus to the rest of the group. Jacob and Alex and their partners had already completed the course. They were on their way to the go-karts, metal water bottles in hand.

"In training, coach," Jacob had said as he turned down pop and held up his bottle. For some reason, he insisted on calling her coach, that, or Vicar Gwendolyn. Jacob and Alex were both running cross country this fall, in anticipation of basketball season where they excelled, especially Jacob. It seems his earlier years of dance classes had turned him into a lanky, yet graceful, b-ball player, his parents had told her.

"Before that, he was more or less a gamer. All he wanted to do was play video games," Dale had explained. "Then Caleb, our oldest daughter, Ashley's boyfriend at the time, noticed him. He encouraged Jacob to try out for the team his freshman year and he was hooked."

"Where's Ashley now?" Gwen asked.

"In New York, studying at Juilliard."

"Impressive," Gwen nodded her head. She remembered Ashley. "And Caleb?"

"He received a scholarship to play basketball at a local university. He's hoping Jacob will join him next year."

Gwen wondered about the "water" bottles Jacob and Alex were toting. Yes, they were serious athletes, but then she had known other "serious" athletes who weren't so serious that they didn't imbibe at times. She knew they both liked to party. Would they be dumb enough to bring alcohol to a youth group activity? One that Jacob's parents were chaperoning? Dumb enough, or over confident in their ability to fool everyone, including his parents? She wondered if she should confiscate the bottles.

"Your turn," Ian called to Gwen. Gwen took aim and hit. The golf ball rounded the curve, went over the hill and into the hole. She still had it.

"Whoa, you sure you aren't a ringer?" Ian asked. He wasn't a shabby player himself. His athletic body nicely filled out the collared white shirt he was wearing. The white brought out the deep tan of his arms. He removed the Chicago Cubs ball cap and ran his hand through his short brown hair. A slight mustache played over his lip.

"You want to put a little money on the next one and find out?"

"Five dollars says you can't do that again," Ian said.

"You're on." Gwen picked up her ball, returned to the tee, placed her ball and hit another hole in one. "Want to go again?" she asked as she pocketed the money. Ian was definitely making this more interesting.

"Too rich for my blood," he said. They proceeded to the next hole. Gwen glanced over and watched Jacob and Alex climb into go-karts. Four more holes to go. Then she would check on them.

Gwen didn't get to finish her game before being called away by a commotion at the go-karts.

"Ian, would you stay with Grace and Josie while they finish?"

"Sure thing. You go ahead."

A crowd had gathered at the go-kart landing. Sure enough, Jacob and Alex were in the middle of the crowd. Gwen arrived as the manager of the go-karts was calling the police.

"What's wrong?" Gwen asked.

"These punks, they were driving erratically. When I told them they needed to slow down or come in, they ignored me. Then they crashed their carts."

"Are they okay?"

"They are, but they won't be. I've called the police. Have they been drinking?"

Gwen looked at the two. Her suspicious were confirmed. "No, they are good kids, part of the youth group."

"Tell that to the cops. Plenty of members of youth groups end up behind bars."

Ian arrived at the same time that a squad car drove up. Officer Liam Kelley again. Gwen wanted to shrink into the ground and hide.

"Gwen," Officer Kelley nodded in her direction as he walked up with his partner.

"You know her?" the manager asked.

"We've run into each other on occasion."

"Tell her she needs to keep her kids under control."

"What happened?"

"These two. They crashed their go-karts. I want them arrested. I think they've been drinking."

"Have you been drinking?" Officer Kelley asked.

"No, sir," Jacob responded. "We're athletes in training. We only drink water and energy drinks."

"I'll see about that." Liam's partner looked into the go-karts. The water bottles that had been sitting in the carts were gone. "There's nothing here."

"I swear I saw them drinking while they were driving. That's in violation of the rules. I want them removed."

"Look, there's minimal damage to the karts. Everyone appears to be okay. Why don't you let it go?" Officer Kelley suggested.

"I want the two of them banned from riding my go-karts."

"That's your right. You can do that. You don't need us for that," Officer Kelley said. "Go on, nothing to see here," he dispersed the crowd.

"You're banned for life," the manager told the two.

"Banned for life? Don't you think that's a bit harsh," Officer Kelley said. "They're just kids."

"For life," he repeated.

"Okay, you heard the man. Get out of here." Officer Kelley walked the two boys out of the area. "You two seem to be getting quite the reputation. I don't want any more calls involving you. You understand?"

"Yes, sir," both boys responded.

"And if you have been drinking—"

"No, officer, we haven't," Jacob interrupted.

"— Let me finish. If we had found alcohol in your possession, that would be an MIP – minor in possession. You don't want that on your record. Might disqualify you from playing basketball. You don't want that to happen, do you? I know, I don't. I look forward to seeing you play again this year, Jacob and Alex." Liam looked over at Gwen. "Now don't be giving your youth minister any more trouble," he told them.

"Thank you," Gwen said.

"Just doing my job," he said as he left.

Once they were gone, Ian came up beside her and the twosome.

"Looking for these?" he pulled out the two water bottles from a bag. The boys looked uncertain about claiming the bottles. "Don't worry. I dumped them." He handed the bottles to the boys.

"Thank you …" Jacob started.

"Don't thank me. Thank your youth minister here. I did it for her, not you," Ian stated.

"Thank you," they both said as they faced Gwen.

"You can thank me by staying out of trouble. You're lucky Ian's the one who found these bottles. I wouldn't have been so kind. Now get out of here. You're also lucky your parents don't know about this." Dale and Ava were in another section of the park. Gwen turned to Ian. "Thank you, though I don't know about letting them get away with this."

"They're just kids."

"Where's Grace and Josie?"

"I sent them to get food with the rest of the youth group."

"Thank you again."

"You can repay me by going out with me."

"Who says I owe you anything?"

"You owe me the chance to get my money back. Are you as good at real golf as you are at miniature golf?"

"Better."

"How about next Saturday at five. We can tee off then, play a round, then go out for dinner. The loser pays."

"That will be you," Gwen stated.

"Then it's a date."

"Sure, I'll meet you there." Gwen walked back to the picnic site where Dale and Ava were busy serving hot dogs to hungry teens.

"What was all the commotion we heard?" Dale asked. "I thought I saw the police."

"You did, but it was nothing," Gwen said.

"It didn't involve Jacob?" Ava looked at Jacob then back at her.

"No, it was nothing. Nothing to be concerned about."

"That's good," Dale said as he handed her a hotdog.

Gwen glanced over at Jacob to make sure he hadn't missed her act of kindness. He owed her now.

Chapter 23

Golfing was just the distraction Gwen needed. Ian seemed nice enough. The other dates just didn't seem right, like there were set-ups, but this one happened so naturally. Ian was practicing his swing when she arrived at the country club.

"Do you golf much?" Gwen asked

"Used to. Not so much now. Not since Mandy. But that could change," he said with a smile.

"Mandy?" Gwen could feel her neck and shoulder muscles tense up.

"My old girlfriend."

"How old?"

"About your age."

"No, I mean, how long ago since you broke up?"

"Oh, a year or so. It's definitely over."

Gwen took a deep breath and felt the muscles relax. Ian was a good golfer. They were evenly matched, both breaking par on the first hole.

"I see you've done this before," Ian commented.

"Once or twice. My parents are members. My dad and I used to golf whenever he had some time off."

"As a doctor, I imagine that wasn't often."

"Not often, but more often than you would think." Gwen climbed into the golf cart Ian had rented. "You know, I make it a point of driving myself on first dates. But, for you, I'll make an exception."

"I'm a very good driver."

"We'll see." Gwen laughed as they rode to the next tee. It was a beautiful Indian summer day. The trees had just started to turn colors. Gwen breathed in deep the warm air, knowing too soon fall would lead to winter. While golfing she forgot about everything else.

No worrying about whether ministry was the right vocation for her. No worry about the youth group or next week's sermon. She could just relax and focus on hitting the ball. They rounded the curve for the sixth fairway and almost ran into another golf cart.

"Mandy, watch what you are doing," the rider in the other cart yelled out.

"Hey, Ian." A brunette with her hair pulled back into a pony tail waved at them, then pulled alongside of their cart.

"It's a mistake, man," Ian said to the man riding with Mandy, "letting Mandy drive. You'll end up in a sand trap or the water."

"Wouldn't be the first time," the man laughed. "I'll take my chances."

"I thought you said Mandy was a good golfer," Gwen said after they left.

"That was golf. I never said she was good at driving the golf cart."

"She's pretty. Who was the man with her?"

"Brian. My ex best friend."

"Your ex best friend, dating your ex girl friend?"

"That's right. It's all in the past."

Ian's game wasn't the same after that. He sliced and sent a ball into the water, then the sand the next hole, not making par either time.

"You're making this too easy for me," Gwen commented as she climbed into the golf cart. "Relax. Everyone has a bad hit now and then."

Ian grunted his response, put the cart in reverse, hit the gas and ended up in the sand trap. Gwen helped him break the cart loose of the sand. Again he hit the gas. This time he ended up in the water.

"Looks like we'll be walking back to the club house." Gwen waited for him to climb out of the cart.

"Sorry. I don't know what got into me. I don't usually drive like this." They pulled their clubs out of the cart and started the walk back.

"You know, if this is your way of getting out of our bet ..." Gwen said.

"No, you win. Anyone who leaves a golf cart in the water automatically loses."

"You've done this before?"

"Just with Mandy, and she was driving." They were both hot and sweaty when they reached the club house. "We can grab a bite here," Ian said.

"I'm not really dressed for the country club."

"We do need to shower and change. You want to meet back here in an hour or so."

"Or we could just do pizza, as we are."

"No, you deserve something better. Meet me at seven."

Gwen showered then picked out a dress to wear. No heels, she decided. That would make her taller than Ian, just in case there was dancing. She slipped on dressy shoes with low heels. When she got back to the country club, Ian was sitting at the bar finishing a drink. He ordered another one, then escorted her to a table, drink in hand.

"You look great," he said as he pulled out her chair.

"You're not shabby either," Gwen smiled. "Do you come here often?"

"As often as I can. First, I came under my parents' membership, but now I've got my own. I'm a bonafide member. This is where I met Mandy. She's a waitress here."

"Is she working tonight?"

"No. I asked. You can have me all to yourself."

Gwen questioned that. It seemed everyone knew Ian. The bartender, other club members, all the waitresses.

"Your usual, Ian?" their waitress asked.

"No. I think I'll try something different. New date, new order." They placed their orders. Gwen decided to go for the steak. She was hungry and Ian owed her.

"I'm not the first person you have dated since breaking up with Mandy, am I?"

"Close, the second."

"Are you sure you're over her? Because it didn't seem like it to me."

"If you are worried about being a rebound, don't. I have tried dating others since then. They just didn't click."

"And now?"

"We'll see," he smiled at her and took a sip from his drink.

Gwen nibbled on the shrimp cocktail and the crab dip Ian had ordered as appetizers and finished off the salad that came with her meal while Ian regaled her with stories about his life. He had gone into the family business and was clearly not hurting for money. He stopped abruptly.

"Is something wrong?" Gwen asked.

"I can't believe it."

"Believe what?"

"The nerve of some people, bringing her here."

"Who? Mandy?"

"And my former friend." Gwen started to turn to see them. "Don't turn around. We'll pretend we didn't see them. Laugh," Ian ordered.

"What?"

"Laugh like I just told you the greatest joke ever. You can do it. You studied acting, didn't you?"

"But that —"

"Laugh." Ian cut her off.

Gwen forced a laugh. The couple approached the table. Mandy had on a sultry low-cut red dress, her hair, freed from the pony tail, hung in curls about her shoulders.

"Ian, nice to see you again."

"Mandy, I hadn't noticed you. And Brian. I didn't expect to see you here."

"Why not? You know we come out here every weekend," Brian stated.

"That so." Ian swirled his drink then took a sip.

"We won't keep you. Enjoy your date," Mandy said. They went to a table in the far side of the room from them.

"Enjoy your date, enjoy your date. She's just rubbing it in," Ian mumbled.

"Why did you come here if you knew you might run into her?" Gwen asked. Ian ignored the question and continued to glare at the couple. "Maybe we should leave?"

"I'm not leaving. If anyone should leave, it's them."

"Then maybe I should leave."

"Do that if you must. Your mother said you could be difficult."

Gwen pulled her head back and frowned. "What does my mother have to do with this?"

"She told me not to give up if you were difficult."

"She did? What else did she say?"

"Nothing important. Mandy doesn't really love him. She's just trying to make me jealous." Ian continued to fixate on the couple. The waitress brought their meals.

"I'll be having mine to go," Gwen said.

The waitress looked at Ian before responding. "Very well then." She took the plate back to the kitchen.

"Don't bother getting up. I can see that you are otherwise occupied." Gwen stood up and waited by the kitchen door for the waitress to bring her meal. She watched Ian finish his drink then order another one, putting up his hand to let the bartender see he needed another round.

At least she was getting a meal out of this one, she thought as she drove home. She was getting better at these dates.

She called her mom on the way home. No answer. "Mom, we have to talk." Gwen left the message on her mom's voice mail.

Chapter 24

Confronting her mom had to wait until Monday morning because of church on Sunday. Gwen decided she needed to sit down face to face with her and this required breakfast at her parents before her mom left for work.

"Mom, what is going on?"

"Whatever do you mean?" her mom responded, pouring her some coffee.

"You know what I'm talking about. All these men, Ian, Wayne, Evan, Roger, Gordon, Leon. You're up to something."

"Is it my fault I have such an attractive daughter that the men just can't keep away from her? You've got good genes."

"Mom, tell the truth."

"Oh, all right," her mom sat down across from her. "Maybe I did have something to do with them."

"Spill it. Tell me everything. Where are you finding these men?"

"I met Ian at the country club. What was wrong with him? I thought he was the perfect gentleman, and he's a successful business man."

"Who happens to still be in love with his ex-girlfriend."

"Oh, her. You're better than her. You could win him over if you just try."

"And what about the other guys? Where did you find them?"

"I didn't actually find them. My friends, they found them for you. It's kind of a club."

"A club?"

"Yes, the Man of the Month club." Her mom lifted her coffee cup and looked at Gwen over the rim. "We're just trying to help you."

"The Man of the Month club? What kind of club is that?"

"The idea is to find someone new for you to date every month until you find the right one."

"Wait. Then how come I met Leon, Roger and Gordon the same month?"

"The girls got a little carried away."

"Let me see if I got this right. You and your friends have been going around town trying to find people for me to date?"

"That's right."

"Mom, what were you thinking?" Gwen jumped up and paced about the kitchen. "You're making me the laughing stock of the whole town. I'm trying to minister here."

"We've been discreet."

"Really? How many men have you approached?"

"Just the ones you met."

"You mean everyone you talked to agreed with this?"

"Most of them. All we had to do was show them your picture. You are photogenic, dear." Laura put her coffee cup down. "And there was the Thunderbird."

"The Thunderbird?"

"The person who finds the right man for you wins the Thunderbird." Laura picked her coffee cup back up to hide behind it.

"Mom, how could you?" Gwen sat back down and put her head between her hands. "This is a disaster. How will I ever be respected as a minister if this gets out."

"It's not that bad, honey. Besides, how are you going to find someone when you are so busy at the church. We're doing you a favor. You do want to get married someday, don't you?"

"Yes, but not this way."

"Why does it matter how you meet as long as you meet?"

"It matters, Mom. I'm not sure why, I just know it does."

"It will make a great story for me to tell my grandkids."

"No, it won't, because you're going to call the whole thing off"

"Why would I do that?" She put her coffee cup down.

"Because I'm telling you to. Because I'm your daughter. Because if you want to have time with any grandchildren I might have, you'll call it off now."

"It's not as easy as you think."

"Why not? It's easy. Just call your friends and tell them it's over. Do it now. I'll sit here until you do."

"And disappoint them?"

"Would you rather lose your daughter?"

"Look, Gwen, you're upset. I understand that." Her mother placed her hand on Gwen's "You aren't thinking this through. Think about it logically. You do want to meet someone, don't you?"

"Yes, I guess."

"And you don't have a lot of time to invest in finding that someone?"

"No, I guess not." Gwen sighed and agreed.

"Then let us do the leg work for you. We'll hunt out eligible men, weed out the ones that aren't right for you, then set you up."

"And that's what you have found so far? I'm not impressed." Gwen folded her arms in front of her on the table.

"You know how hard it is to find eligible men your age? The good ones are already taken. If you don't move fast, there won't be any available. You'll have to wait until they start getting divorces."

"Not funny, Mom."

"I'm not being funny. Let us help you." Laura reached for her daughter's arm.

"You aren't going to let this go, are you?"

Her mother shook her head no and smiled.

"Okay. But I have the final say about anyone you chose."

"You always did, dear."

"I mean before I even go out on a date. I have input."

"Welcome to the club." Her mother stretched out her hand and they shook on it.

Chapter 25

Liz Schultz lived in an old farm house outside of town. The white structure sat on the top of a hill, overlooking the long driveway that meandered its way from the county road to the barn that served as a garage.

Liz waved to Gwen from the front porch then called her to join her. Gwen sat down in the unoccupied rocking chair.

"I see myself, years from now, sitting on this porch, waiting for my grandchildren to visit. You can't miss visitors from up here. Don't miss much of anything."

Gwen nodded her head in agreement. The porch offered a panoramic view of the country outside of Cascade Falls. From this vantage point, you didn't even know a city was nearby. She relished the moment of peace as she gazed across the horizon and sipped the cold water Liz provided. The trees were in their full glory and so was Liz as she gazed about her domain. The only reminder of Liz's surgery was the wrap she still wore about her head, hiding the bald spot. On Gwen's last visit Liz had shown her the peach fuzz that was populating her head.

"As soon as this gets long enough, I'll have the rest of my hair cut to match it. Thus, aside from the scar hidden in my hair, there will be no evidence of my brain tumor." That and a slight hitch in her gait now and then was all that remained to remind her of the surgery. The tumor had affected her balance. Liz was confident that too would disappear, fade into some semblance of normalcy.

"I like this time of day. The kids at school, chores that are going to get done, done. I get to sit and watch for the kids to get home and make the trek up the driveway." Gwen knew that Liz still had limited energy since the surgery. Gwen knew from previous visits if she entered the two-story house, she would find piles of laundry that never seemed to find their way upstairs to their rightful home.

"Terry keeps assuring me he will carry it upstairs but for some reason that never happens," Liz had said with a smile.

"Is there anything I can do to help?"

"Just keep me company on this beautiful day. That's enough. Seems a shame to not share all of this beauty."

There would also be dishes piled in the sink, waiting their turn to be placed in the dish washer, Gwen figured. She had tried insisting that Liz let her help with this, only to be denied again.

"It's the least I can do," Gwen had said. Some days the sink was empty and the dishwasher humming when she arrived. Other times, not. She knew Liz did what she could and Terry filled in the rest where he could, but it was hard for him, working and trying to keep up with the kids and chores. Hard for both of them.

On good days, Liz greeted her from the porch. Other days Gwen found her sitting on the couch, eyes struggling to stay open. She didn't stay long on those days. She didn't want to take up what little energy Liz had, wanted her to save it for her children and husband. Today was a good day.

"And maybe you'll come to visit me. We'll be little old ladies, sitting in our rocking chairs, swapping stories and swatting flies. You will come back to visit me, won't you?"

"Every time I'm in town."

Liz smiled at this response, then breathed in deep and closed her eyes. "Smell Autumn. Autumn air has its own fragrance, don't you think? Kind of fresh and wild and at the same time, old — old with the passing of another year. The smell of decay as leaves fall from the trees and form a bed on the ground." She leaned back and continued to breathe deeply.

"I know I'm not fooling anyone." Liz kept her eyes closed as she spoke. "I don't know how many years I have left. I won't be around to see my children grow up, much less any grandchildren. But I see it now in my mind's eye. I see a future that might have been but will never be. I want to believe in that future for as long as I can. You'll help me believe, won't you?"

Gwen didn't know what to say. "How?" she asked.

"Just play along with me. And when I'm ready, help me face reality, whatever that might be. Can you do that? It will be our game."

Gwen agreed, not quite sure what she was agreeing to. She would play along. She was good at that.

She stayed until Liz's children came home from school. Leia came running, excited to share her news about the day. TJ dragged his backpack in the dirt.

"TJ, pick up that backpack," Liz scolded from the porch. "I don't know what gets into that boy." She accepted hugs from her daughter and forced them on her son.

"Time for a snack," Liz said. This was Gwen's cue. Liz escorted her children into the house. Gwen climbed into her car and made the trek back down the dirt driveway, onto the county road and into the reality that was Cascade Falls.

When Gwen asked about helping Liz around the house, Pastor Joe assured her that was not her job.

"You're a minister, not a social worker."

"But couldn't we arrange for some help?"

"We can and will. But when you visit, you aren't there to pick up the house or cook meals or do the laundry or any of the other chores that you think need doing. That might imply a criticism."

"I'm not being critical, just trying to be helpful."

"This isn't about what you mean, but how Liz might interpret your actions. It's about what she needs, not what you want to do. Cleaning her house might make you feel good at her expense. It might be a convenient way to avoid what's most important."

"And what's that?"

"Sitting with someone who is confronting her own mortality. Just being with her. Feeling helpless along with her before the vastness of eternity. Not doing, not rescuing, not running away from the enormity of it all. Perhaps that is what she most needs from you."

Gwen understood what Pastor Joe was saying. She had heard similar words in her counseling courses. But that had been in theory. This was reality, in the form of a flesh and blood woman, a wife and mother, who was faced with losing everything. Doing the laundry would be easy. This was not.

Chapter 26

Gwen sat outside at Adelle's, drinking her sour lemonade and swatting flies. She was getting used to this.

"Flies at a picnic," Adelle had said the last time she had come.

"What?"

"Flies at a picnic. That's how Teresa of Avila described distractions in prayer. They are annoying. You can't get rid of them entirely but you can't let them distract you from the main feast in front of you. Just swat them away if you have to. Otherwise ignore them."

"Easier said than done," Gwen said as she brushed away another fly.

"Tell me about your prayer life," Adelle instructed.

"Not much to tell. I talk. God listens, or at least I hope he listens."

"What do you talk about?"

"Whatever is going on in my life."

"And what does God say?" Adelle leaned back as she spoke.

"God doesn't usually say anything."

"Then maybe you aren't listening."

"Oh, you know, there are people who insist God's always talking to them, but it's usually them talking to themselves, telling themselves it's God when it isn't."

"How do you know it's not God?" Adelle cocked her head and raised an eyebrow.

"Because God doesn't work that way."

"Not for you."

"No, not for me." Gwen took a sip of lemonade.

"How does God talk to you then?"

"In silence. Sometimes I just get a feeling, a sense of presence." Gwen smiled to herself then looked over at Adelle. "How do you pray?"

"I pray in so many different ways. Over the years we change, our prayers change. Sometimes I just poke around."

"Poke around?"

"Yes, you know, like a doctor poking around to find the spot that hurts."

"What happens when you find that spot?"

"I look for the hurt, the unhealed pain, and I keep poking at it till it heals. When I was younger, your age, I had a lot of unhealed spots. I'd poke until tears surfaced, then I'd cry and give the tears to God. I still find those spots now and then, but not so much anymore. I guess that comes from a life of brutally looking for any unhealed parts in my soul."

"And God heals them?"

"Sure does. You want to try it sometime?"

"I guess, when I get some time to pray."

"No. I mean now. Is there a spot that hurts?"

"Seems there's so many of them, I wouldn't know where to start."

"You just begin. God takes care of the rest. Sit in silence and see what surfaces. Try it."

Gwen closed her eyes and tried to poke around in her mind the way Adelle had told her to. Something was there but she couldn't quite find the right spot. "Nothing," she said after a while.

"That's okay. You're just a beginner. Sometimes at the beginning God gives us experiences, enough to whet our desire for him in prayer. Then God calls us further into prayer, where the consolations are fewer. The important thing is that you keep showing up. If you do that, quiet your mind and listen, God will show up in ways you don't expect. Can you do that?"

"I'll try." So far Gwen hadn't made much progress. There was so much going on in her head. She just couldn't clear a path to God.

This month when Gwen met with Adelle, she was back in her garden. So many of the flowers and plants had been cut back and lay in decay. All that was left in her vegetable garden was squash and pumpkins. The pumpkins were overrunning the garden, with vines spreading through what remained. Adelle was gathering the squash into baskets, leaving the pumpkins to rot on the vines.

"Why?" Gwen asked. "Why aren't you picking the pumpkins?"

"No need for them. Like pumpkins rotting on the vines in the garden. Some writer used that metaphor once for African-American women, back in the days around slavery, I believe. I can't remember the writer. Probably messing up the quote. The meaning remains."

"What is the meaning?"

"That for women, African-American women of that time, their gifts weren't recognized. They weren't allowed to fulfill their potential. All the giftedness, all the talents of generations of women were left rotting on the vine because they weren't allowed to use them. Times have changed. So much more opportunity for women of any color. But I believe in God's economy, there is no waste. God gathers up all people, not a one is wasted."

"How can that be?"

"You forget. We are dealing with God here." Adelle sighed. "But a wasted life is a terrible thing." She picked up her basket and walked back into her home. Once again, Gwen had been dismissed.

Chapter 27

The aroma of apples brewing into cider and donuts warm from ovens filled the air. Gwen breathed in the crisp fall air, felt it burning cold in her lungs. One of the things she missed while living in Chicago. The leaves just turned brown and dropped in the city. You had to drive for miles to enjoy an apple orchard. Unlike here where it was just a short twenty-minute drive from church.

She was getting pretty good at driving the church van, not something she had aspired to, but, as long as she had to do it, it was good she knew what she was doing. Gwen found thoughts rumbling through her head as she drove the church van to the orchard. Running the youth group was also not something she had aspired to either. She didn't like being a glorified babysitter and party planner. She wanted to do ministry.

"You are creating opportunities for ministry to happen," Pastor Joe had told her when she complained. "Sometimes our most powerful ministry experiences happen when we least expect them. Openness is everything."

Yeah, right. So how come he wasn't spending all his time with the youth group? At least with the young adults she had someone else doing the planning. All she had to do was show up. And then she had the Bible study. At least she had the opportunity there to talk about Jesus. These kids, though … Whenever she tried to talk to them about God, they tuned her out. She could read it in their faces. Most were attending the Lutheran high school. Maybe they were getting enough religion. Maybe … As soon as she had a church of her own, she would do what most pastors do and find someone else to run the youth group.

She understood why it was so hard to get and keep good youth ministers. You had to have a heart for this age group. That wasn't her. She'd yet to start the vlog she had wanted to begin, another source of frustration. Pastor Joe had her running, between home visits, hospital visits, youth group, Bible study, drama team, young adults, meetings, and, oh yes, preaching and writing for the church newsletter. There was little time left to even begin thinking about a vlog, much less start one. You wanted to have a series of ideas for vlog posts before you started lest you run out after only a few. She was thinking one a month would be enough, but was it? At this rate, St. Luke's would never make it into the 21st. century, at least not on her watch.

And then there was her mother and her "club." And Sam. And Adelle. Who had time to eat and sleep, much less start something new? And then all the instructions to take care of herself, pray every day, exercise, eat healthy, find balance between work and home. How do you do that when where you live is also where you work?

"Some days you just do the work at hand and try to maintain some sense of balance," Pastor Joe told her. She wondered how he had lasted so many years — clearly because he had left youth group to someone else.

Gwen pulled the van of chattering teens onto the grounds of the orchard. Tonight they were doing a haunted corn maze and hay ride. Next month it would probably be a Thanksgiving meal, then a Christmas party. So predictable. Then winter activities. At least it got her out of the manse, out in nature. Gwen breathed in the smells, allowing them to fill her nostrils. Maybe it wasn't so bad.

As the sky darkened, she rounded up the kids for the wagon ride.

"Aren't you coming?" she asked Dale and Ava from her perch atop a hay mound.

"We've done enough of these," Ava said. "You enjoy the ride. We'll be here at the campfire with hot cider."

Gwen hadn't thought staying behind was an option. Too late. The wagon had already started. Someone had to stay with the kids and make sure they behaved.

"This is so lame," she heard Jacob complain to Alex and anyone else within hearing range. "The haunted corn maze? Like that's going to scare us. They'll probably have someone dressed up like Freddy Kreuger with a chainsaw."

"How do you know?" Grace asked.

"Because I've done this for four years now. It's always the same. They'll have ghosts and fake bats and creepy noises. Are you scared, Graceless?" Gwen knew Grace hated it when Jacob called her that.

Then why don't you stay home, Gwen wanted to say, but bit her tongue. "Well, don't spoil it for the rest of the group," Gwen told him.

Jacob certainly was a challenge. She didn't know why he kept coming to youth group, except his parents probably made him. That and Cherie and Marie, the Townsend twins. It seems they couldn't get enough of Jacob and Alex, and Jacob and Alex enjoyed the adulation.

Gwen leaned back into the hay and peered up into the sky. Something else you didn't get in Chicago. Too much light pollution. The stars were nowhere near as bright and not as many of them. She could see why God told Abraham his descendants would be as numerous as the stars. On a cloudless night out in the desert, over three thousand years ago, the stars probably were as numerous as the grains of sand. It must have been a spectacular display.

Gwen tried to block out the shrieks and chatter of the teens as she contemplated the universe. She had to admit, it was pretty lame. With all the horror movies with special effects that kids see, how could the owners of the orchard compete? She was surprised she didn't hear more complaints from Jacob. Then she realized she didn't hear his voice, hadn't heard his voice for at least five minutes. That wasn't like him. She could usually hear his voice as he kept up a steady chatter. Jacob was a trickster, much like his namesake in the Bible. He was always playing pranks, cracking jokes. She had not known him to be quiet for this long unless he was up to something.

Foolish her. She had figured he was trapped on the wagon. How much trouble could he cause? Apparently, she was wrong.

She looked around the wagon. Jacob and Alex were nowhere to be found. They must be planning on trying to scare everyone. Think. Her brain zoomed. If you were a teenage boy what might you do as a Halloween prank? Toilet paper a house? Eggs? No, that wouldn't work.

"Incoming," she heard male voices shout from the maze, then screams as something came flying at them. "Dinosaur poop! Cover your heads!" the voices shouted.

Gwen stood up to better see what was happening and felt something splat against the side of her head and ooze through her hair. Egg.

Girls were screaming, boys were laughing and tossing broken eggs at each other. The driver pulled the wagon to a halt. "What's going on back there?" he yelled as an egg hit him in the shoulder. Another egg hit one of the team of horses, spooking it. Both took off at a run.

"Whoa, whoa," the driver kept calling to the horses, trying to calm them down as the screams continued.

"We're all going to die," one of the Townsend twins cried.

"Cool." Trevor and his buddies kept laughing. Everyone was holding on tight. Gwen was almost thrown off the wagon. She landed back on the hay mound, egg sliding down the side of her face and onto her shoulder. They rounded a corner at full speed, going off the path and hitting the maze. Workers who had been hiding in the corn maze jumped out of the way of the wagon. When they realized what was happening, one jumped onto the wagon and helped the driver slow down the team. Once the horses were brought to a halt, two other workers came out, holding onto Jacob and Alex. Their hands were tied together in front by twine from a hay bale.

"That was awesome," Trevor shouted. "Best haunted ride ever." He gave Jacob and Alex a thumbs up and a high five from his spot on the wagon. Some of the girls were crying as they tried to wipe egg out of their hair and clothing.

"Do you have any idea how much trouble you two are in?" The driver jumped out of the wagon and walked over to them. He raised his fist like he was going to hit them. Instead he came within one inch of their faces as he yelled. "You could have killed someone." He continued to glare at Jacob and Alex as he yelled. "Who's responsible for these two?"

"Ah, that would be me," Gwen climbed down from the wagon and joined the group around the boys.

"I want them out of here. You can walk the rest of the way back through the maze."

"But what if we get lost?" Gwen asked.

"All the more time to think about what they have done."

"I didn't do anything," Gwen complained.

"You're the one who was supposed to be keeping these kids out of trouble. You can share their punishment. And when you get back, I want you to leave. You'll be banned from coming back."

The threesome walked after the wagon, following the path as best they could.

"Do you two plan to be banned from every place in Cascade Falls before your senior year is through?" Gwen asked them.

"Don't worry, coach. I can find our way back. I've done this maze so many times, I could walk it in my sleep," Jacob assured her.

"That's not what I asked. And we may be sleeping here if we don't find our way back."

"What are you going to tell my parents?" Jacob asked.

"I doubt there will be much more to say after the wagon driver fills them in."

"Oh, yeah. He was pretty pissed off."

"I'd say you're lucky to still be alive. What were you thinking?"

"Come on, coach. We just wanted to make the ride more exciting. You saw how lame it was. No one was going to be scared by those people hiding in the maze. We've all seen it before, done it before. You heard Trevor. It was awesome."

"How awesome do you think it will be if the police are called?"

"He won't do that, will he? No one was hurt," Alex asked.

"And if there are any damages, how awesome will it be when you have to pay them? You owe me a sweatshirt." Gwen pointed to the yellow stain on her shoulder.

"Yeah. That might not be so good," Jacob admitted.

"And what if someone had fallen off of the wagon and been hurt? Or if the wagon had tipped over when the horses took that turn so fast?"

"Hitting the horses wasn't Jacob's idea. I did that. I'm sorry. I guess I got carried away," Alex said.

"Well, you're lucky, both of you, that no one got hurt. You'll have to answer to your parents for this. I can't keep it from them like I did the last time."

"Yeah, thank you for that," Jacob said.

"And this is how you repay me? I thought you had learned your lesson."

"Gosh, coach. Haven't you ever felt like you just had to do something, anything, to shake things up a bit or you might explode?"

Gwen did remember feeling that way back when she was Jacob's age.

"It's like, you're trapped in this town, in high school, even though you're ready to move on. You're stuck for one more year. I wish I could leave the way Ashley did, but no one's going to let me skip senior year to play basketball."

"I thought Ashley graduated."

"She did. She just did it through online courses, graduated a year early. My grades are not good enough for me to do anything like that."

"Then you need to make the best of this year, work hard, play hard, get that basketball scholarship."

"Lord know that's the only way Jacob here will get into college." Alex punched his buddy in the arm.

"Hey, you're not much better," Jacob responded, punching Alex back.

"And please stay out of trouble, or you will end up spending your senior year in jail."

"I'll try, coach. It won't be easy."

"Nothing in this life that is worthwhile is easy," Gwen told him. They walked in silence for a while, the stars their only light to guide them.

"It was fun though, you have to admit that," Jacob said.

"You should have seen the look on your face when that egg hit you," Alex said to Gwen. Both boys laughed.

"Our best prank yet," Jacob agreed.

Gwen shook her head and sighed, resisting the urge to laugh.

Chapter 28

"Okay, ladies, listen up. There's a slight change in plans," Laura brought the meeting of the Man of the Month club to order.

"Why? What's wrong?" Margie asked, a forkful of cake suspended in mid-air.

"Gwen knows."

"What? How did that happen?" Hattie asked.

"I bet it was Wayne. His mother never could keep a secret," Bernice said.

"Never mind how she found out. That doesn't matter," Laura said.

"Sure it matters. We need to know whose guy had loose lips. I'm sure it wasn't Leon," Margie said.

"If you must know, it was Ian," Laura said.

"Ian? Your Ian. We love Ian. He's perfect," Margie said.

"And that slight brush of mustache. So cute, not that I notice those things. We should have known he was too good to be true. I guess it's over now," Bernice added.

"Okay, so he wasn't perfect. What matters is that Gwen knows," Laura said.

"Does that mean this is over? No more club meetings? No more cake?" Margie asked.

"No, there's just going to be a few changes."

"Such as?" Hattie asked.

"Well, Gwen wants to have some say in who she dates."

"Sounds fair to me," Hattie said.

"And she wants to come to our meetings."

"All right by me," Margie agreed.

"And she wants to be in on the Thunderbird," Laura rushed the words, hoping to slip them by the group.

"Okay … what?" Bernice said. "Did you say she wants in on the Thunderbird? How is she going to do that? Is she going to be picking men to date too? I'm not giving up one of my months. Besides, it's not fair. Of course she'll pick her guy. We won't have a chance."

"She says she'll give each of your guys a fair shot. What do you say? She is studying to be a minister. She wouldn't lie to us."

"I don't know," Hattie said as the others shook their heads.

"Hey, look, it's the only way I could get her to agree to this. It's either let her into the club or close down."

"Okay, if you put it that way." All agreed

"Great. I knew you would see reason. I'll get Gwen."

"She's here?" Margie asked.

"Sure. I didn't want to spring her on you till you had a chance to get used to the idea." Laura called out to the kitchen. "Gwen, you can come out now."

Gwen came, an open bottle of wine in one hand. She looked around the room, uncertain of her reception. No one was smiling. "Does it help that I brought wine?" she asked and held up the bottle.

"It helps." Bernice took the bottle, looked at the label, nodded her head in approval and poured herself a glass. "So how do we know you won't cheat?"

"I promise. I'll give each guy a fair shot," Gwen said.

"What's wrong with my Leon?" Margie asked.

"Nothing. Leon, Leon is great. He's a great guy."

"He's still in the running, isn't he? He tells me he still has a chance."

"Ah, Leon. He's just, he's too good for me. I mean, he's a great guy. He deserves someone better."

"He is a great guy," Margie agreed.

"How is this going to work? We already have all of the months assigned," Bernice stated.

"That's okay. I'll give up mine. Or, if Gwen happens to find someone on her own, then the bet's over," Laura said.

"Hey, no fair. I told you …" Bernice started.

"But we always said we would continue until Gwen found Mr. Right. Besides," Laura shrugged, "what's the chance of Gwen finding Mr. Right on her own?"

All three laughed and nodded in agreement and took another sip of wine.

"Hey, I'm right here," Gwen said.

"We know, dear, but really, how far have you gotten on your own? If not for us you wouldn't have had any dates yet. Name one man you've found on your own since being here."

Gwen opened her mouth as if to speak, then closed it and shook her head. "Okay, you've got me there."

"You're too picky," Hattie said. "What was wrong with Wayne? You didn't even give him a chance?"

"He brought his mother on our first date."

"So he has a good relationship with his mother. I think that's a plus in a perspective relationship."

"He has a weird relationship with his mother. What twenty-six-year-old man would bring his mother on a date? Especially the first date?"

"If you had given him a chance …"

"What was wrong with Ian?" Laura asked.

"Yeah, we all liked him. He's so cute and clever," Margie said "We thought for sure that he was the one."

"He's still hung up on his old girlfriend, that's what's wrong."

"He would have gotten over her in time. You just didn't try hard enough," Laura said.

"And he drinks a lot."

"Nobody's perfect. You are too picky," Laura said as she took a sip of wine.

"Look, Mom, everybody. If this is going to work, you have to accept it when I say no. All right?" She looked at the four but got no response. "I have veto power, right? Or this isn't going to work."

"Okay," everyone agreed.

"Good. So who do you have next for me?"

"That's Margie's month. Okay, Margie, who do you have for my daughter?"

"That's hard to say. It's hard to come up with someone better than Leon."

"Try," Laura said.

"Okay, how about Jason?"

"Jason, the guy from the mini-mart?" Laura asked.

"Yeah, that Jason."

"I don't know. He's kind of cute, if you ignore the hair lip," Bernice said.

"Hair lip, no way," Gwen said.

"I told you she's too picky. And you being a minister and all. You shouldn't be judging people based on appearance," Margie said. "Besides, the hair lip's not that noticeable. Some would consider it distinctive."

"Okay, good point," Gwen agreed. "Just no hair lips." She thought for a moment then added, "And no one shorter than five six and no fatties."

"Now wait a minute. Do you realize how shallow you are sounding?" Laura asked.

"Okay. You show me their picture. Oh, and I guess I could date someone who's overweight, as long as he has a kind soul."

"That's more like it," Laura said. "Let's see who we can come up with for Gwen." Laura continued to sip her wine as names were put forth.

Chapter 29

November brought Albert, a hillbilly with no front teeth. December, James, who overdosed on cocaine in the bathroom. Another awkward opportunity to talk to Officer Kelley.

"Where are you getting these people?" Gwen asked as she turned down date after date.

"You've already turned down the best ones. July, August, September and October," Hattie told her. "We are fishing in a limited pool."

"Maybe we should just forget it," Gwen said.

"And give up on my baby? No way. There has to be someone out there for you," her mom said. "You've been going to the singles' gathering. Isn't there anyone there?"

"The ratio of women to men is something like five to one and the last few times those men were Leon, Roger, and Gordon."

"Just asking."

"Trust me, Mom. I won't be heartbroken if we give up."

"And end the club? No way," Margie said.

"Okay, so who do we have for January?"

"My guy," Hattie handed her a picture. "You're going to love him. His name's Norman. He works in construction. He's a hunk."

"Okay, so what's wrong with him?"

"Nothing."

"Hattie." Gwen scowled.

"All right. He has a slightly crazy ex-girlfriend. But don't worry. The restraining order should take of her."

"Restraining order?"

"For her, not him. He's a complete gentleman."

"Are you sure he's over her?"

"Sure. He's the one who broke it off."

"Okay. Have him call me." At least now there was no subterfuge. No more strange men showing up at the singles dinners or youth group activities and asking her out.

January was crucial if she was to have a date for Valentine's Day. She had already missed out on New Year's Eve, spending it alone in the manse with Sam. She didn't want to miss Valentine's Day too.

She had settled into a semblance of a routine at St. Luke's. Home and hospital visits Monday and Wednesday afternoon. Bible Study Tuesday night. Other meetings, Monday and Wednesday nights. Youth Group, Sunday nights. Instead of a meal for November, she had the youth group serve a meal at the local shelter. Then they did a toy drive for Christmas. Once basketball season started, Jacob and Alex were much too busy with the sport to cause trouble at youth group. She almost missed the excitement of their pranks. She attended all the local games, sitting with members of the youth group or other church members. Jacob was good, so graceful on the floor.

Every now and then she would run into Officer Kelley at the game as he and his partner would put in an appearance. It was nice to see him under circumstances that didn't involve a crime or the resemblance of a crime.

Gwen fed Sam, then threw on a winter coat over her dress. She had high hopes for this date.

"Hopefully I'll be late," she told Sam as she left. She was giving Giglio's another chance. There were only so many nice restaurants in Cascade Falls. If she eliminated every one where she had a bad date, there wouldn't be any left.

Norm met her in the foyer, helped her with her coat and escorted her to a table with a gentle touch of his hand. He was large, but muscular from all of the heavy labor involved in construction. He seemed uncomfortable, out of place. She liked that in him. He wasn't brash at all, but was soft-spoken and gracious. He ordered a bottle of wine for both of them and calamari. He suggested the linguini with clam sauce.

"Do you come here often?" Gwen asked.

"No, just special occasions. But when I do come, I get the linguini."

Gwen smiled and dipped a piece of bread into olive oil. "I could make a meal out of the bread."

"You have to save room for cannoli for dessert."

"I'll make sure I have room."

"Norman!" Gwen heard someone call his name.

"Don't bother about that. Just my old girlfriend. They won't let her in. The restaurant manager knows about her."

Gwen glanced out the window and saw a woman shouting and pounding on the window.

"Just ignore her. She'll go away soon enough. If not, the police will escort her away."

Oh, good. Another date that involved the police, Gwen thought. It was hard to ignore the noise, but then it got quiet.

"See, I told you she would leave. Wine?" Norm poured her another glass of red wine. "Tell me about yourself."

The woman from outside showed up beside their table.

"How did you get in here?" Norm asked.

"I slipped in through the kitchen. I still have friends here."

"You used to work here?" Gwen asked.

"Yes, before this loser lost me my job." She nodded at Norm.

"You lost the job on your own."

"No help from you. Who is this slut?" she glared at Gwen. "I'm Alice. Your date's fiancé."

"She's not my fiancé."

"You promised. Bought me a ring and everything."

"That was before I realized you were crazy."

"Come back to me, Bubba." She leaned down and squeezed his face. "We were good together. It could be good again."

"Alice, I'm on a date."

"That skinny skank? What's she got that I don't have?"

"She's not crazy. Do I have to call the manager?" Norm motioned to their waiter.

"Don't bother, I can let myself out. I know the way. But you," she pointed at Gwen. "You stay away from my Norman, if you know what's good for you." With that she picked up the pitcher of water and poured it over Gwen's head. Gwen gasped from the icy blast. Then Alice threw a glass of red wine in Norm's face. The manager rushed over, trapped her arms behind her back, then handed her to the bartender who escorted her out the door.

"It looks like you have some experience with this," Gwen commented.

"More than I like to admit," the manager told them. "You could press charges."

"No, we won't do that. She's just a little upset," Norm told him and sent him away. "I'm so sorry," Norm told Gwen. He handed her his napkin to dry her hair. She excused herself and went to the restroom where she spent fifteen minutes drying her hair and dress under the hand blower. When she came back, Norm was gone.

"He said he had to make sure Alice got home okay," the waiter told her.

"Right. Don't tell me, he left me with the bill."

"No, he paid for it with his credit card. Said anything you wanted you could have." Gwen ordered the steak pizzaiola dinner to go, along with cannoli. At least the dinner wasn't a total loss. She sat down to finish her glass of wine while waiting for her meal, then noticed Ian and Mandy at another table. Ian waved at her, then got up and came over.

"You're back with Mandy," Gwen commented.

"Yes, thanks to you. If you hadn't helped me realize I still had feelings for her, I never would have recognized the truth. Let me do something for you." Gwen started to say no when Ian took his card out of his pocket and wrote a name and number on it. "Now that

Mandy has broken up with Brian, he's available. He's a great guy. You'll love him."

"That's okay. I don't want anyone else who's just broke up with someone."

"Call him. You'll be doing me a favor. Besides Valentine's Day is less than a month away. You don't want to be dateless on Valentine's Day, do you?"

"You just want me to date him so he doesn't try to get Mandy back."

"That is part of the plan, but he really is a great guy. Can I tell him you'll be calling?"

"I don't know."

"Think about it." Ian pressed his card into her hand. Gwen looked at the number. February was her month. This time she was going to do it her way.

Chapter 30

Liz was in her kitchen, gazing out the window at her backyard when Gwen arrived. The backyard encompassed an acre of farm land that had been overrun by nature from years of neglect. Snow sparkled in the sunlight. The smell of cinnamon tea filled the cheery space.

Gwen had feared the drive up the long driveway, had almost begged out of coming till Liz assured her it was plowed and passable. Gwen's small Ford Fiesta was not the best on ice and snow-covered roads, but at least it had front-wheel drive. Her dad had made sure of that when he bought it for her.

Liz stood up to get Gwen a cup then poured the fragrant tea into it from a wrapped tea pot where it had been steeping. Her hair, set free from the scarf she usually wore, framed her face in soft brown waves.

"Not as long as before my surgery, but a vast improvement, don't you think?" Liz had said that the first time she had uncovered her new "do" for Gwen. Then her hair had been the same length as Gwen's. "Twins," Liz had joked. Liz had continued to let her hair grow out so now it had passed the length of Gwen's hair. Liz ran her fingers through her hair, smiling as she relished the texture.

"I'm envious," Gwen said.

"Of what? My hair?"

"It's so naturally curly. I always wanted curly hair. Instead I got this." She pointed at her straight cut.

"You could always get a perm," Liz suggested.

"Not the same."

"Funny how we always want what we don't have. When I was younger, I wanted straight hair, like Jennifer Aniston's. I burned my hair using straighteners. Now I'm just happy to have hair."

The house was picked up and tidy. Liz's mom and sister took care of that. When it became clear that she couldn't keep up with the housework, they had stepped in, despite Liz's protests.

"Just until I'm stronger," Liz had said when she told Gwen about it. Gwen was glad she had stayed out of this. Pastor Joe had been right. It wasn't her place. Only Liz didn't seem to be getting stronger. Since the first few months at home, she appeared to be getting weaker. Her balance was worse and she tired more easily.

"My mom and sister, they want to be with me all the time. It's exhausting just having them here. They think I might fall."

"Isn't that possible?"

"If that happens, all I have to do is push this button." Liz pulled a medical alert necklace from where it was hanging under her shirt. Liz had resisted getting the alert device. Gwen remembered that from her last visit. Something must have happened to make her give in. Perhaps the threat of her mother coming over and staying all day. Gwen knew she would agree to pretty much anything to avoid that herself.

"Mom's trying to get me to move in with her. Says it's too much work for Terry, taking care of me and the kids."

"Is it?"

"I'm not helpless. Not yet anyway." Liz turned her face away from Gwen and stared out the window. A doe and two fawn were in the snow-covered field, foraging for food. "I want to stay here as long as I can. Is that selfish of me?" Liz turned back and looked Gwen full in the face, her eyes brimming with tears.

Gwen returned her gaze, struggling to know what to say. "If it were me, I'd want to stay with my family."

"That's what I want. As long as I'm able. As long as I'm not too much of a burden."

Gwen reached for her hand and squeezed it.

Chapter 31

Gwen entered the small room off of Adelle's porch and living room. A small space heater blasted warmth into the room. This was Adelle's inside space for spiritual direction once the weather turned cold. There were large windows looking out over the garden, where you could watch the changing seasons. There were three seats and a small table with a candle that Adelle lit. Gwen figured the extra seat was for when Adelle met with couples.

"That's the Elijah chair. At Jewish Seder meals they leave a seat for when Elijah returns. It's also the Jesus seat. Or for anyone you would like to have join us, literally and figuratively."

Gwen didn't want to invite anyone to these sessions. She didn't want to be here herself. Pastor Joe insisted she continue.

"When you look at the snow-covered land, what do you see?" Adelle asked.

"Snow. Cold. What am I supposed to see?"

"It's up to you. I see potential."

Gwen waited without responding. She knew no response was required. Adelle would keep talking regardless of whether she responded or not.

"This is the fallow time. I love this time. A time of rest before new life and spring. Under that bed of snow, new life is teeming, just waiting for the opportunity to break forth."

"I thought the land was resting." Gwen decided to challenge her.

"It is. Rest can be very productive. Sleep is productive. While you are sleeping your brain is busy healing parts of your body, renewing cells. Sometimes you have to stop in order to get anything done."

Was she baiting her? Gwen refused to take the bait. She was putting in her time because she had to. Didn't mean she had to spend any of her mental energy on these meetings. She had so much going on in her head as it was. All she wanted was to get back to her office and get some work done.

"Can you rest, truly rest in the Lord?" Adelle asked.

"I guess so." Gwen was forced out of her reverie. Did Adelle realize her mind had been elsewhere? That she hadn't heard the last thing Adelle had said?

"Let's try. Right now."

"Right now?" Gwen shifted in her chair. "What are we trying?"

"We are going to rest in the Lord. Let God cover you with a sacred blanket of snow."

"If you say so." If she expects me to go out into the cold and lay in the snow, I'm out of here, Gwen told herself.

"Just place your feet in front of you. Place your hands palms up in your lap. Close your eyes and let me do the work."

Gwen was no stranger to quiet meditation. She just wasn't that good at it. She preferred reading Scripture and reflecting on it or using prayer books. Still, those times when she did manage to be still in the presence of the Lord were productive. She didn't know why she didn't do it more often.

"Imagine that snowflakes are gently falling on you, coating you with a layer of white. Stay still lest you knock any of it off of you. Let them fall. One by one. One snowflake at a time. Each snowflake is unique, like the people who come into your life each day. Are there concerns you are carrying? Burdens? Unfinished tasks waiting to be done? Let them pile on you till you are not sure you can breathe."

This is crazy. Gwen struggled to keep from shifting.

"Feel their weight, pulling you down. The snow keeps falling. Soon it becomes a mound and you can no longer move. But you feel safe and warm under its depth. There is freedom in being trapped by the snow. You push aside all of the work and responsibilities and just breathe, just relax. You forget about all the people and their concerns. You forget about yourself, till all is gone, buried under snow."

Gwen wondered when this would be done. Gwen jumped as a splash of water hit her face. "What was that?"

"It's spring," Adelle laughed as she continued to splash water on Gwen's face. "What is waiting to be born in you?"

"Nothing. You're crazy. Nothing is waiting to be born in me. I'm getting out of here. I don't care what Pastor Joe says." Gwen picked up her purse.

Adelle smiled. "That's what I want you to reflect on. In your prayer time. While you sleep. What is God bringing forth in you?"

Gwen let herself out, not bothering to schedule another meeting.

Chapter 32

After a few days, Gwen called Brian and asked him out for coffee. Coffee was good. It was long enough to figure out whether he was worth investing any more time in but not so long that it got awkward if it didn't go well. When coffee went well, they went out to a movie and had drinks afterwards. And when that worked, she had a date for Valentine's Day.

Brian was all right. He was a lawyer at Ian's dad's business.

"So you and Ian work together? That must have been awkward when you were dating Mandy."

"We try to keep our business and social life separate, but yes, it was. I thought I would be fired or at least forced to quit."

"How did you manage?"

"You know, Mandy's a beautiful girl, but she's also a gold digger. I think she just used me to get Ian to propose. Why settle for a lawyer when you can marry the owner of the company."

"Did he propose?"

"That's my understanding. No date has been set yet. Ian's dad isn't happy about him marrying a waitress."

"How sad."

"For whom? Mandy's getting a rich husband and Ian's getting what he deserves."

"What's that?"

"Mandy."

"And what about you? What do you get out of this?"

"That's yet to be seen." Brian smiled and leaned over and kissed her.

Brian invited her to the Valentine's Day dinner and dance at the country club.

"Won't Ian and Mandy be there?" Gwen asked.

"What's that to us?"

Gwen agreed. She was pleased to realize she could wear her heels with Brian and not worry about any awkwardness on the dance floor. She wouldn't tower over him. If nothing else, even if Brian wasn't Mr. Right, he was Mr. All Right, and she got to go dancing.

Gwen wasn't surprised to learn her mom and dad were going to the Valentine's Day Dance too, along with her mom's friends and their husbands. It was one of the more popular events at the country club.

She hung on to Brian's arm as she introduced him.

"Is that February?" she heard Margie ask.

"It's not fair," Bernice said.

"But look how happy she is," she heard her mom say as she slipped away with her date. Ian and Marcie were there, as expected. Even Leon and Gordon were there with the women they were dating.

"Leslie's a member," Leon informed her when she greeted them.

Gwen didn't feel herself relax until dinner was over. "Finally, a meal that isn't interrupted," she said.

"What were you saying?" Brian asked.

"Nothing. Let's dance."

Brian was also a good dancer. The music was ballroom dance music. Waltzes, two steps, tangos. Gwen appreciated the dance lessons her mother had insisted on her taking years ago. After a few dances, Leon asked to cut in. She wished she could slip off her shoes to get closer to eye level.

"I know we were kind of a thing," Leon started.

"One date, Leon."

"I just want you to know, I'm with Leslie now, so what we had, it's over."

The dance couldn't get over soon enough for her. She thanked Leon for the dance and rejoined Brian who had been dancing with Leslie. From the foyer the sound of arguing was heard in the silence between songs.

Gwen couldn't make out the words, but recognized Ian's voice.

"I will not quiet down and you can't make me." Mandy's voice sounded through the room.

More muffled sounds came from Ian.

"I don't care if I make a scene. I'm leaving."

Mandy came into the room and searched the crowd until her eyes rested on Brian. She walked over to him and put her hand on his arm.

"Brian, you have to take me home."

"Mandy, I have a date. What about Ian?"

"What about Ian? That no-good jerk. Please, Brian. You have to help me. Who else can I turn to?"

Brian looked over at Gwen and shrugged. "What can I do? Can you get a ride home with your parents?"

"It looks like I don't have any other option."

"Thanks, Gwen. You're the best." Brian left with Mandy clinging to his arm.

Gwen went over to her parents' table and explained she needed a ride.

"Sure, honey. … That jerk," her mom said and hugged her.

"The club's still on," Margie said to Bernice. They clicked their wine glasses while Hattie frowned at them and nodded in Gwen's direction.

"Can't you see the girl is hurting?" Hattie said.

"No, I'm okay," Gwen said. "Who's got March?"

Chapter 33

Gwen visited Richard every other week. He appeared to enjoy her visits, though his mom, not so much. She sat in the room with them and frowned as they talked.

Each time Richard kept telling her how God was healing him, but Gwen didn't see any improvement. If anything, he was getting weaker. He also told her about these natural cures he was trying, organic food, special beans. He insisted she take a bag home with her on her last visit. She was surprised when he called a week later and asked her to bring them back.

"I have to go see Richard again," she told her mom as she prepared to leave.

"Didn't you just see him last week?"

"Yes, but he gave me these special organic beans that he's been eating. Says they are going to cure him, that and no salt. Apparently he ran out and wants me to bring them back."

"If he didn't have enough, then why did he give them to you in the first place?"

"Because he's crazy," Gwen said as she went out the door. She didn't mind seeing Richard, but it was inconvenient. She had to drop other things in order to do it. Gwen was all too aware of the pile of paperwork on her desk. She wasn't ready for Bible study that night and this was her week to preach. She figured she would drop the beans off then leave.

She let herself in as was her custom. Richard's mom was not pleased to see her. Gwen handed her the beans then faced Richard.

"You shouldn't have given them to me if you didn't have enough." She tried to keep any anger out of her voice.

"I thought I had enough."

"Well, you do now." Gwen stared at him for a moment, unsure what to say. He motioned for her to sit down.

"Sorry. I can't stay. I have too much to do. I'll come back next week," she told him.

"Thank you for bringing the beans," Richard replied.

Gwen hurried back to church and finished her lesson plans for that night.

The next day she was surprised when Pastor Joe called her into his office.

"I just got a call from the funeral director. Seems Richard Dalton died last night."

"What? That can't be. I was just there yesterday."

"He wanted you to do the funeral."

"But it can't be." Gwen sat down. "Were the beans just an excuse so he could see me one last time?"

"What beans?"

"He called and wanted me to bring back the beans he had given me last week. I thought it was weird at the time, but I did it. He was insistent that it had to be yesterday. He wanted me to stay but I was in a hurry to get back."

"You must have brought some light into his life."

"Maybe, I guess. I should have stayed and talked to him." Gwen shook her head as she allowed the reality to sink in.

"You had no way of knowing. Do you want to do the funeral?"

"I guess, if it's all right with you."

"The funeral director says it's just going to be a graveside service. That's all Richard wanted."

"In the snow?" Gwen looked up at Pastor Joe.

"Yes, in the snow. Here's the number. Call him to work out the details."

Gwen took the number from Pastor Joe and returned to her office. How could she have been so oblivious? The service was set for Friday at eleven. There was only going to be immediate family. Gwen assured him that it would be a short service because of the cold. Just a few words over the grave site. That's how Richard would have wanted it. The body would be placed in the ground in the spring.

Gwen got out the Lutheran book of prayer and read the prayers for the grave site. That would work.

It was bitter cold at the graveside. The funeral director placed a few chairs. Richard's mother shivered on one. Everyone else huddled around shivering. There were only a handful of family members in attendance. Gwen read through the service, then shared a few words of remembrance.

"Richard, as you all know, was a pilot. He loved flying planes. Felt close to God when it was just him and the sky. It has been hard for him, being grounded all these years by MS, but through the last months, he was convinced that God was healing him and he was going to walk again. He was right. God was healing him, just not in the way Richard expected. And now he is able to walk again as he joins God in his heavenly home."

Afterwards Richard's nephew approached her. "What you said about my uncle, thank you. It means a lot to me, knowing he is out of pain."

"You're the journalist," Gwen said. "Your uncle was so proud of you, kept telling me about you. Have you graduated yet?"

"Next spring." He shivered as he reached for her hand to shake it. The rest of the family hurried away into the limo provided by the funeral home. Gwen was left alone at the grave site. She shivered as she said her own private goodbye to Richard, apologizing for not being understanding on her last visit. She shook her head as she reflected on how inadequate she was, then walked away.

Chapter 34

Was someone knocking? Gwen looked up from her laptop. Grace and Josie. They knocked so gently she almost missed it. Gwen tried to be available after school for youth group members to drop in. So far no one had taken advantage of the time so she used it to get caught up on office work.

"Josie, Grace, good to see you. Sit down. What can I do for you?"

Josie walked slowly to a chair and sat down. Grace followed behind her.

"We were thinking …" Josie started.

"We want to start an environment club, HOPE - Help Our Polluted Environment. We were hoping you would help," Grace jumped in.

"An environment club? It's a great idea, but I'm not sure it fits my job description."

"Care for God's creation. Pastor Joe talked about it in his sermon last week. We want to do something about it," Grace said.

"We just read online that plastic has been found in raindrops. Do you know how frightening that is? It means there's most likely plastic in the water we drink every day. We are drinking plastic. That's scary. We have to do something," Josie added.

"Don't you need to have a teacher as your advisor?"

"You would qualify. We checked it out. The principal said it was okay for you to do it," Josie said.

"Oh, you checked it out."

"And didn't you talk at Youth Group about how we need to care for all of God's creation?" Grace added. "This would be a great way to do that."

"But who will take over when I leave?"

"We'll find someone. We need someone good to get people involved, someone like you," Josie said.

"I'm flattered," Gwen responded, "but I hardly consider myself—"

"If you got involved, other members of the youth group will join," Josie said.

"Anyway, maybe you could get the young adults to help out too," Grace suggested.

"I don't—"

"Please. You'd be great, and it's so important," Grace said.

Gwen looked at both of them, trying to resist. "What would we do?"

"We'll take care of it. All you have to do is show up," Josie said.

Show up. That she could do. Easy peasey. What's another time commitment? "When do you meet?"

"I knew she would be willing to do it," Grace jumped out of her seat.

"I didn't say yes, yet," Gwen objected.

"But you were getting ready to, weren't you?" Grace insisted.

Gwen looked at the girls again. "Okay. I'll do it. But you'll take care of everything, right?"

"Right. We'll plan the meeting. You just show up," Grace said. She waited patiently while Josie stood up and walked to the door.

Now what had she done? What was she thinking? But how could she say no to the two of them? One more thing to keep her from starting her vlog. The year was already more than half over. If she didn't start it now, she might as well forget about it.

She decided to forget about it.

Pastor Joe didn't seem the least bit upset when she told him. "That's just how church life is. Like family life. Sometimes you have to set aside your own plans to do what is in the best interest of the church."

"But the vlog was in the best interest of the church."

"Was it?"

"I just couldn't fit it in with everything else I was doing." How could Pastor Joe not see this?

"And that's okay. Sometimes it takes all you have just to tackle the job at hand. Doesn't mean it wasn't a good idea. Doesn't mean you wouldn't have been able to do it if you had more time here, more than a year. The first year in a church is pretty much just for getting to know people, traditions, history. Once you get a feel for a place, you can start introducing new ideas and programs."

"Or," Gwen drew out the word. "Or, the first year in a new place is the perfect time to start new initiatives, before inertia sets in. While people are still getting to know you and open to change."

"Some do hold that school of thought. I guess you can test it out when you get your first church."

"If I get my first church."

"Why would you say that?"

"Because ..." Gwen shrugged and sighed. "First, I have to complete this internship. Sometimes I wonder whether I'm cut out for church ministry."

"That's what you are here to test."

"You won't feel like a failure if I decide I don't want to be ordained after this year?"

"Gwen, when I do marriage prep with a couple, my goal isn't to get them married. That may be the couple's goal. Once engaged they often become so focused on the wedding that they fail to think about the marriage. My goal is to slow the wedding train down, get them to think whether this is what they really want to do. Are they really right for each other? Have they talked about kids, finances, hopes and dreams for the future? If in the process they break up, I don't feel like a failure. I've done what I'm supposed to do. If I stopped a marriage that would likely end in divorce from happening, I've done my job. It's the same thing with interns. If a person really isn't meant to be ordained and I help them recognize it, I've done my job.

This isn't about me, it's about what's right for you, what God is calling you to."

"But, if that happens too often, won't the seminary stop sending you interns?"

"That's for me to worry about, and I'm not worried. However, if someone who shows a potential for ministry becomes discouraged and walks away without giving it a fair trial, then, yes, I might feel I have failed that person." Joe paused. "Ultimately, it's all in God's hands."

"Isn't that a way to excuse yourself of responsibility? Say it's in God's hands and don't do anything?"

"You are making this difficult. No, that's not what I mean at all. Remember—"

"I know. Pray like everything depends on God, work like everything depends on you."

"Just because it seems cliché doesn't mean it isn't true."

Right, Gwen thought. Now if only she knew what God wanted her to do, then she could work like it all depended on her.

Chapter 35

Liz's mother greeted her at the door, not Liz.

"Mrs. Thurston. I didn't …"

"Liz is very weak, but she wants to see you." Gwen followed her into the living room where Liz sat up on the couch, propped up by pillows, her legs extended the length of the couch. Liz smiled and instructed her mother to bring them some tea.

"And those sugar cookies you made, Mom." Her mother paused as if to protest, then left the room. "That ought to keep her busy for a while.

Gwen sat down on a chair next to the couch. She pulled herself forward to keep from sinking into its softness.

"We don't have a lot of time. Seems there's never enough time."

"Are you okay?"

"I get to see my children every day, sleep in a bed with my husband. I'm blessed."

Her mother arrived with a pot of tea and a plate of sugar cookies. She poured tea for both of them, then Liz dismissed her.

"She thinks I'm going to talk of death. That's why she doesn't want to leave me alone with you. She doesn't want me to talk to you or anyone about dying. She wants me to move back home so she can take care of me."

"Are you going to — talk of death, that is?"

"What is there to talk about? Everyone dies. I would gladly go if only it didn't mean leaving Terry and the kids. I've had enough of this life." She attempted to pull herself further up on the couch from where she had slid down. She reached for the small devotional Bible that was sitting on the coffee table and pulled out the prayer cards she had shown Gwen while in the hospital.

"Remember these," she handed them to Gwen. Gwen glanced at them.

"Yes, I do."

"When it hurts too much. Not just physical pain. I can handle that. But the thought of leaving all those I love. I picture myself being held in God's arms or flying on the wings of an eagle and I am comforted."

Gwen looked at the prayer cards. On the outside, she said the appropriate words and prayed with Liz. On the inside, they gave her little comfort. Her friend was going to fly away and leave her here, alone. Once again, she was left with her inadequacies.

Chapter 36

Grease oozed from the bun as Gwen sunk her teeth into her cheeseburger, then wiped her mouth. She savored the mixture of grease and fat, hamburger and melted cheese. So far, so good. Matthew, her date, was appropriately charming. Well dressed, but not overdressed. He had a good sense of humor. What could go wrong? Gwen kept looking for an ex to show up, or a mother, or for him to start talking about something bizarre. So far, nothing. That was good.

She had decided on Burger Barn for this date. No big expectations, just burgers, fries and conversation, as befitted a non-occasion.

"You know, I know about your mom's club," Matthew said.

"Of course, Margie told you." Margie was Matthew's aunt. It was her month.

"No, I knew before that. I contacted her about it."

"How did you find out?"

"Not hard. This is Cascade Falls after all."

"Right." Gwen sighed and took another bite of burger. Marcie had been right. It had been a mistake, moving here, living in a fishbowl.

"I told my aunt I wanted to meet you."

"You did? Why?"

"Because I thought we might be able to help each other."

"How so?" Gwen put her burger down and leaned back.

"My aunt doesn't know I'm gay."

Neither did she. She thought her "gaydar" was better than that. How could she have missed it? Gwen didn't respond, waiting to hear out Matthew's proposal.

"My mom and aunt are always trying to fix me up with dates. I heard about the Man of the Month Club and thought, your mom is trying to fix you up too. Why not date each other? My mom and aunt will be happy. Your mom will be happy."

"But you're gay."

"They don't know that. As long as we give the appearance of going out with each other, our families will stop trying to set us up with other people. It's a win-win situation."

It was a thought. Gwen was getting tired of the club. She just wanted to focus on her ministry. This would make that possible.

"And if someone comes along that I'm interested in dating?" Gwen asked.

"I'll step aside. We could be each other's 'wing man.' What do you say?"

"Would you be my date for St. Pat's Day?"

"Of course."

"Deal." Gwen reached over and shook his hand. Now she would have a date for events and men would stop hitting on her. What could go wrong?

Chapter 37

St. Patrick's Day is a big bar day, or weekend, or week, depending on when March 17 falls on the calendar. If it falls during the week, some places take advantage of this to have specials on both weekends, before and after the actual date, as happened this year. Gwen was looking forward to the day. The youth group was having a St. Patrick's themed party on the Sunday before. The singles group was having a party with another church singles group on the Saturday after. That left her free on the actual day to do what she pleased.

She and Matthew were going to start at the downtown brewery for Irish music, a pint of Guinness, and appetizers, then on to a local bar with a dance floor for dinner and dancing, meeting a group of Matthew's friends. The band didn't know any Irish tunes, but they played Irish music in between sets over the sound system. Gwen led the group in a rendition of "When Irish Eyes are Smiling" and "My Wild Irish Rose." Then Matthew took the floor to sing "Danny Boy."

The band made up for not knowing any Irish music by playing great dance music. Gwen and Matt were on the dance floor throughout each set. Sometimes Matt's friends joined them, other times they were the only ones on the floor. After two Irish car bombs, Gwen was over any inhibitions about dancing in front of a group of people. She got up and let the music take her where it would.

Gwen wasn't surprised to see Officer Kelley walk in with his girlfriend. She was getting used to running into him everywhere she went. Besides, what self-respecting Irish man would miss a pint on St. Pat's Day?

She smiled as Liam and his date entered the dance floor. She waved at them and invited them to join their circle of dancers. They were more sedate than Matthew's friends, dancing alongside them but not joining their circle. She was not to be outdone as they took turns dancing across the floor from one side of the circle to the other. When the band switched to a slow dance, Matthew asked Liam's date to dance, leaving her with Liam.

"Having fun?" Gwen asked him.

"How could I not be? I'm dancing with two of the prettiest colleens in the bar."

Gwen loved that Liam put on an Irish accent. It was becoming. She laughed then tried to get him to do a turn, bumping up against him as she attempted to go under his arm. "Loosen up. Or do you need another Guinness?"

Next to them, Matthew was gracefully escorting Liam's date about the dance floor.

"See how it's done," Gwen nodded in their direction.

Liam pulled her close, keeping her from attempting any more fancy steps. "Your partner is quite the dancer," he commented. "But when I dance, I lead."

"So lead then."

"You have to follow. Relax." Liam put his hand in the small of her back and continued to hold her close till she stopped resisting. He loosened his grip as they rocked back and forth together. Gwen laughed and looked into his eyes. It was fun to be able to look up into her partner's eyes, something that wasn't possible with other dance partners she had. Their eyes locked. She felt her head whooshing from the alcohol. She continued to look into his eyes, her head whirling, her heart beating hard against his chest.

She excused herself as soon as the music stopped and rushed to the restroom. She sat on the toilet seat as the world whirled about her. She didn't know whether she was going to throw up her corned beef dinner. Was it the dinner? Or the drinks? Or the dancing? Or her new dance partner? Or all four of them? She wished the room would stop spinning.

"Are you okay?" She heard the voice of her nemesis, Liam's girlfriend. Only she didn't know she was her nemesis. She didn't even know her name. She was just Liam's girlfriend and thus in the way of her getting that which she most desired. Or not? Please room, stop spinning. She didn't know what she wanted.

"I'll be fine as soon as the room stops twirling." Gwen tried to stand up then ended up on her knees before the porcelain goddess. Liam's girl waited patiently for her to finish. Gwen wished she would leave. She thought she was better than this, thought she was better able to handle her drinks. Guess not. She didn't want anyone around to witness her shame.

But Liam's girlfriend didn't leave. She handed her a wet paper towel when she came out of the stall.

"Here," she said. "Wet your face with this. You'll feel better."

Like anything would help her feel better. Gwen went to the sink and splashed water on her face. "It was those Irish car bombs."

"Tell me about it. That's why I don't drink them. Liam, though. He's an Irish car bomb himself."

"What are you talking about?"

"You keep fooling around with him and you won't know what hit you." She handed her a dry paper towel. "I'm Angie. Liam's fiancé."

"Gwen," she said as she dried her face with the paper towel.

"I know," Angie said. Why did everyone know her?

"Fiancé? Liam never said anything about being engaged."

"He never does," Angie said.

Liam and Matthew were waiting for them back at their table.

"We were beginning to think we would have to send in the SWAT team to check on you," Liam said as Gwen sat down.

"Just girl talk," Angie said. "Time to go," she told Liam.

Liam looked like he was going to disagree then changed his mind. "You sure you're okay?" he asked Gwen as he stood up.

"I'll make sure she gets home okay," Matthew told him.

"What were you thinking?" Gwen asked on the drive home.

"I'm thinking you've had too much to drink to drive home." They had met at the brewery then drove to the bar in Gwen's car. Matthew got his car from the brewery, left her car there then drove her home. "You can get your car in the morning."

"No, I mean making me dance with Liam."

"No one was holding a gun to your head. You looked like you were having a good time. Remember. I'm your wing man. You are clearly into that man. Who wouldn't be?"

"In case you didn't notice, he has a girlfriend. A fiancé. The woman you were dancing with."

"I didn't see a ring on her finger."

"Well, she told me. She warned me to back off. As if I was going to take another woman's boyfriend."

"As long as there's no ring, he's fair game in my book."

"What kind of a person does she think I am? I'm a minister in training after all." Gwen's words were cut off by a hiccough.

"You keep telling yourself that. You didn't dance like any minister I know."

"What was wrong with my dancing? King David danced in his underwear before the Ark of the Covenant. It's an expression of joy."

"Too bad we didn't stay longer. That dancing in your underwear thing. That sounds like fun."

"Ha ha, I wouldn't do that."

"Are you sure? One more car bomb and who knows what you would have done."

"What was in those drinks anyway?" Gwen spent the rest of the drive home in silence, trying to keep from a repeat of the incident in the bathroom.

Her head was throbbing. She pleaded for someone to turn off the beating in her skull. "Wow, what did I do last night?" Gwen muttered.

"Precisely what I want to know." Her mother's voice broke through the pounding.

"Mom, what are you doing here?" Gwen forced her eyes open enough to see her mother standing at the foot of her bed.

"Checking on you. Don't you remember you have a ten o'clock appointment?"

"Oh no. What time is it?" Gwen fumbled for her phone.

"Ten thirty."

"Can you cancel it?"

"Already did. Now get out of that bed and tell me what happened."

"Sorry, Mom. St. Patrick's Day. You know." Unfortunately, her mother did know.

"I heard all about it. Seems you made quite the spectacle of yourself on the dance floor, then puked in the bathroom."

Gwen dragged herself out of bed. That was the awful taste still in her mouth. "If you'll excuse me, I need to take a shower. How did you get in here anyway?"

Her mom held up a key chain loaded with keys. "Church secretary. Remember?"

And to think she was the one who had helped her mom get the position.

"Mrs. Wickersham was the first to call Pastor Joe this morning." Wickersham was the chair of her internship committee. "I waylaid her for now. Told her Pastor wasn't available, but word will get to him soon enough."

Gwen dreaded those committee meetings. She was always met with a laundry list of complaints. Not by the whole committee, just Mrs. Wickersham. One Wickersham was enough to scare anyone out of ministry. She fumbled her way to the shower. And now she had given Wickersham even more ammunition in her arsenal against her.

Chapter 38

The welcoming cup of coffee and smell of cinnamon rolls didn't fool her. Gwen knew that an invitation to brunch by her mother was rarely a good thing. Still, she couldn't avoid her, especially when they worked together. Might as well get it over with the semi-controlled environment of her childhood home.

"I know what you are up to." Her mother sat down across from her.

"I'm not up to anything. I'm just trying to survive my internship." Gwen understood her mother had an ulterior motive. Especially when she realized her dad wasn't going to be there because of a meeting at the hospital. This was going to be another one of those heart to heart talks where her mom did all of the talking and she sat and fumed. At least she was getting breakfast out of it.

"Gwen, this is Cascade Falls. I'm a church secretary. You can't keep any secrets from me."

Gwen gulped. What did her mom know? She and Matthew had worked out an elaborate plan to fool everyone into thinking they were a couple. Did her mom know?

"I know Matt is gay. His aunt knows he is gay. All of Cascade Falls knows he is gay. Who do you think you're fooling?"

"If Margie knows, then why did she fix him up with me?"

"Because he asked her. He's her favorite nephew. Margie figured if he doesn't want her to know, she would wait until he is ready to tell her. Besides, I think there's a part of her that wants to believe differently."

"She thought I could 'turn' Matthew?"

"Maybe."

Gwen sat in silence at her parents' kitchen table, the sight of so many conversations over the years, some pleasant, some not so pleasant. She ranked this one among the not so pleasant ones.

"Don't you want me to be a grandmother?"

"Mom, you already have grandchildren."

"Might as well not for all I see them."

"What do you want me to do, Mom? I tried. I even cooperated with your crazy scheme."

"I just want you to be happy."

"And find someone to marry and settle down in Cascade Falls."

"Would it hurt for one of my four children to live nearby?"

"Not going to happen, Mom. Can we please call off your gang of yentas?" On her better days, Gwen remembered watching musicals with her mom. They had once danced in the kitchen singing, "Matchmaker," from Fiddler on the Roof. Marcie had been part of the fun back then. That was almost twenty years ago. It wasn't fun now that her mom was trying to be a matchmaker in real life.

"Is this what you really want?"

"Yes, Mom, it's what I really want. Please. No more set-ups. No more men. Just let me finish out my internship in peace."

"If that's what you want, baby, I want it too." Her mother reached for her hand and clasped it in assurance.

Then why didn't Gwen believe her?

"So, we're done?" Hattie asked after Laura explained the situation at the next meeting.

"Heck no. We just have to be sneakier," Laura said.

"I don't know if I can do that," Bernice said. "It just doesn't seem right."

"Look, if you don't want to be part of this …" Laura said.

"And give up on the Thunderbird?" Bernice sighed. "Okay, I know no good can come from this and Gwen will end up hating all of us, but I'm in."

"Me too." Margie held up her wine glass. "Here's to being sneaky."

"Here's to Gwen," Laura added as they clinked glasses.

Chapter 39

Repeated attempts to get through to Liz on her phone with no response. What was going on? Then she received a no longer in-service message. When she called Terry's cell phone, again no answer. Finally she reached him on their landline, calling after eight o'clock, after the children were in bed.

"I'm sorry to bother you so late," Gwen began.

"No, I'm sorry for not calling you back," Terry said.

"I'm trying to set up a time to visit Liz."

"You'll have to call this number." Terry read off a number. "I'm sorry. I can't talk now."

Gwen didn't recognize the voice when she called. "I'm trying to reach Liz Schultz. Her husband said I could reach her at this number."

"This is her mother. Liz can't come to the phone," a hushed voice answer. "She's staying with us."

"Would I be able to visit tomorrow?"

"I guess that would be okay," the voice responded and gave her the address.

Gwen looked up the address on her phone. A city address. She arrived a little after one o'clock to a small, ranch style home in a cul-de-sac. There were several cars in the driveway so she parked on the street. She was surprised to see Terry there. He didn't talk to her, turning away when he saw her. Liz's mother brought her into a room where Liz lay on a hospital bed. Quiet music played in the background. From the other room she heard sobs and voices talking.

"I can't bear to see her like this." She thought the voice was Terry's.

Liz's mother held Liz's hand then drew her hand across Liz's cheek. "I'll leave you alone with her."

Gwen took Liz's hand, unsure what to say or do. She had never been in a situation like this before. Didn't know what to do. Liz's breath was labored. Her face gaunt. She appeared to be unaware of Gwen's presence.

"The last thing to go is hearing," she remembered from one of her classes. She figured she should say something. Instead she remembered the passages from Liz's prayer cards. She imagined Liz, cradled in loving arms, embraced by God, then soaring in the sky like an eagle. Then she saw Jesus, holding Liz's limp body in his arms. He looked at Gwen for but a moment, then they both faded away.

Gwen wanted to scream. "Wait. Come back." Then she noticed Liz's breathing change. Was she dying? What right did she have to be here? She called Liz's mom into the room. Her mother immediately took Liz's hand and caressed her face again, calling to her daughter through tears. Other family members came into the room. They didn't notice Gwen slipping out of the room, leaving the family alone to grieve.

The funeral was four days later. Liz's parents had never accepted her becoming Lutheran. They had not wanted a Lutheran service for their daughter, but Terry prevailed. He wanted both Pastor Joe and Gwen to do the service. Gwen had protested when Pastor Joe asked her to participate.

"I knew her for such a short amount of time. Surely there are other people more qualified to speak about her life."

"But you are the one they want, both Liz and Terry."

How could she say no to a dying request of a friend?

On a cold day in Lent, amidst a gathering of friends and family, Gwen joined her pastor in celebrating the life of Elizabeth Schultz, wife, mother, daughter, friend. Liz wanted her body cremated and the ashes buried on their property so she could see her children coming and going and someday, her grandchildren.

Pastor Joe did the sermon. Gwen shared a short eulogy at the end. She mentioned the time they had spent together and the two prayer cards. "Towards the end, I was comforted knowing Liz was being held in God's loving embrace and in the end, God carried her home." The service ended with the hymn, "On Eagles' Wings."

"You did fine," Pastor Joe told her afterwards.

"Then how come I feel so terrible?"

"You never get completely used to burying church members you have come to love. It doesn't necessarily get easier, especially for someone so young. You bear up and push through. And afterwards …" Pastor Joe paused.

"What happens afterwards?"

"After the service, after everyone has gone home, you allow yourself to feel the full weight of your loss."

"That sucks."

"Maybe, but it's a privilege, being there with someone at the end of their life, a gift. It was Liz's gift to you. It's a privilege, being allowed into other's lives where they face their God, helping in that relationship."

"Right now, I don't feel so privileged."

"You will, eventually. But first you grieve."

Gwen went home, sat on her couch with Sam next to her, and grieved as she pondered the mystery of a life gone so young.

Chapter 40

The Breslin Center at Michigan State University was electric. So much energy. So much excitement. St. Luke's basketball team had made it to the state finals for their size school. Gwen had driven the youth group, joining with half of the school. This was a first for their small high school. There had been years where they hardly had enough players to have a team, much less a championship team. Jacob and Alex had led the team this far and inspired them. Even though they were clearly the stars, they knew the value of teamwork and worked well with the rest of the team so that they had more boys trying out for the basketball team than ever before, giving their team a depth of players. It was a magical season. One Gwen had never seen in her years at Cascade Falls.

She sat next to Dale and Ava, the proud parents. Next to them were Alex's parents, Taylor and Micah. Taylor had met Micah while doing missionary work in South Africa. Alex was their youngest. They had moved to Michigan when Alex was in third grade. His older brothers and sister had since gone on to college and moved out, leaving him the last in the nest.

Jacob moved with the grace of a dancer.

"He takes after his mother, not me," Dale said. "I was never that good at sports. I was okay, just not good, not like Jacob."

Jacob wouldn't admit that the dance lessons he had taken as a child had anything to do with his success on the court. Alex was the stronger athlete, taller and faster than Jacob. What Jacob lacked in speed and height, he made up for in grace. They were going to need all of that and more to beat the other team in the finals, a Catholic lineup from Grand Rapids. Neither could count on God being on their side because both counted on God being on their side. They would have to win with a combination of hard work, talent and luck.

The teams were closely matched. Gwen found it impossible to sit back and relax. Maybe she needed Adelle's snow. The teams kept passing the lead back and forth as quickly as they passed the ball. St. Luke's was up by two points at halftime. Gwen got up to stretch her legs and get something from concessions.

"Good game." Liam came up behind her in line.

"The best. But nerve wracking. I wish they would just pull ahead and get a comfortable lead so I can relax."

"What would be the fun in that? You can relax later."

Gwen laughed as she edged forward in the line. "You here by yourself? You could join us."

"No. I'm here with Angie." Liam pointed to the stands where Angie was reapplying lipstick. She waved at Liam and blew him a kiss, then glared briefly at Gwen. Liam didn't notice, but she did.

"Oh, yes, the fiancé. How is that going? When is the wedding?"

"Who said she was my fiancé?"

"She did."

Liam looked back up at Angie. "Look. It's not like it appears."

"And what is that?" Gwen made it to the front of the line and ordered a Coney dog.

"I mean, we've been going together for a long time, but we aren't engaged."

"I'm not the person you need to be saying this to."

"It's complicated."

"Always is." Gwen paid for her Coney dog and joined some of the youth group who were standing together outside the court.

"Have you got everything worked out for Earth Day?" she asked Grace and Josie.

"Working on it. We still have some details that need to be worked out. We'll finalize them at our next meeting," Josie told her. Josie lost her balance and almost fell, spilling the coke she was holding. Gwen and Grace both held her up. "Guess I better clean that up."

"Don't worry about it," Gwen told her. "I'll clean this up. You go sit down."

Josie had a hard time climbing steps yet she insisted on attending basketball games and climbing up to her seat. Most times she refused any offer of help. She refused any suggestion of special treatment. She also continued to refuse braces to help her. She wouldn't talk to Gwen or anyone about it. Not even Grace. Josie had been diagnosed with Charcout-Marie-Tooth Disease years ago. It ran in her family. Charcout-Marie-Tooth, or CMT, was a neurological disorder that affects the nerves in the arms and legs and weakens muscle. Gwen knew that as Josie's CMT progressed braces would be inevitable, unless they had some major breakthrough. Surgery could also delay that but that was a painful process. Josie's parents were here too, watching over their daughter from the sideline of her life.

"You've got quite the daughter," Gwen had told them before.

"Don't we know it," her dad had agreed.

"I just wish she would let us help her," her mother said.

"She's independent, like her mom," Josie's dad had said. Her mom hadn't agreed.

Gwen finished her Coney dog, then wiped up the spilled drink before heading back to her seat.

The second half was just as tense as the first, even more so as the minutes counted down. Going into the fourth quarter, St. Luke's was ahead by ten, their first double-digit lead the whole game. A couple of turnovers and some fouls, and they were back behind by two points.

"Hard to know who to root for," Fr. John from St. Paul's in Cascade Falls slipped into the seat next to hers. She had met him through the local ministry association. He was friends with Pastor Joe and had been sitting with him during the first half of the game. "Do I root for the Catholics or the home town team?"

"No question in my mind," Gwen answered.

"I heard about this Man of the Month Club. Can anyone get in?"

Gwen gasped, her attention diverted from the game. "How do you know about it?"

"Small town." Fr. John laughed.

"You can't date."

"Not me, but I know someone."

"It's over and done with, Father."

"That's not what I hear."

"Then you hear wrong."

"Well, if you change your mind … You'd like my guy."

"Not changing my mind." Gwen frowned. What was her mom up to now? Then Jacob landed a three-pointer putting St. Luke's back in the lead and diverting her attention back to the game.

Thirty seconds left to go. All of the time-outs had been used. St. Luke's lost their possession of the ball. If they could just keep Catholic Central from scoring, they would win. Foul. The Catholic Central player made one of the two shots, making it a tie game.

Alex took the ball out, passed it to Jacob who ran it down the court. Alex ran to the basket. Jacob threw a long shot. Alex tapped it in right before the buzzer. What a relief. Gwen didn't know how much more of this she could take.

The talking was non-stop in the church van on the way home. Gwen stopped and treated them to ice cream. They went to the high school and joined the crowd waiting for the team bus to get back. They followed the players into the gymnasium where the celebration continued. The band played the school fight song then the coach spoke to the crowd, thanking them for their support. The crowd started to thin out when the team went to the locker room, but the gym was still half full when they came out in their street clothes.

Gwen excused herself and walked home to the manse, leaving others to keep the party going. Time to work on her sermon. Maybe she could work this win into it. What was she thinking? Of course she would work this into it.

Chapter 41

Something was buzzing. Was it time to get up already? She reached for her cell phone and saw she had missed a call from Pastor Joe. One o'clock. Why would he be calling so late?

"Gwen, I need you at the hospital. Meet me in the ER," he told her and hung up before she even had a chance to ask why.

She arrived at the ER and went to registration to ask for Pastor Joe when she saw Jacob, sitting by himself in the waiting room.

"Never mind," she said. "Just tell Pastor Joe I'm here." She stepped over to where Jacob sat, head in hands, his right foot bouncing.

"Jacob? What's wrong? Why are you here?" she asked.

Jacob looked up with a vacant stare, as if he didn't know her. "It's Alex."

"What about Alex?" Gwen sat down next to him and rested her arm around his shoulder.

"Pastor Joe is with him. They wouldn't let me in the ER."

Pastor Joe came into the room through the doors to the ER and approached. Dale and Ava came in from the street, through the emergency room entryway followed by Alex's parents. They converged on the spot where she sat with Jacob.

"Where's Alex?" his parents asked.

"He's hurt," Pastor Joe told them.

"How badly? Can we see him?" Micah, Alex's father asked.

"Not just yet. They are working on him."

"He's alive, isn't he?" Taylor, Alex's mother asked.

Pastor Joe took a breath before answering. "He is, but it's serious."

"Jacob, what happened?" Dale asked his son.

"We went out on our bikes," Jacob told him.

"Why were you riding your bikes so late? We thought you were home," Dale said.

"I couldn't sleep, so I called Alex. We met at the park."

"Jacob," Dale lowered his voice. "Were you drinking?"

"Just a couple beers. We figured as long as we weren't driving it would be okay. Neither of us could sleep. It was such a nice night. We didn't think it would hurt to be out on our bikes."

They were interrupted by the arrival of Officers Nash and Kelley. Pastor Joe was called to the reception desk for a phone call.

"Alex can have visitors now," he told Alex's parents.

"What about me? Can I see him?" Jacob asked.

"Not yet." Pastor Joe shook his head. "Besides, I think these officers might have some questions for you."

"That's right, son," Officer Nash said. "We do have questions for you."

"Can't it wait?" Ava asked.

"Let them do their job," Dale told her, wrapping his arm around her waist and taking her aside.

"Did you get the license number of the car that hit you?" Officer Nash asked.

"No. It all happened so fast and it was dark."

"Can you describe the car?"

"Metallic blue, four-door."

Officer Kelley stepped forward while Officer Nash wrote notes. "We found beer bottles at the scene of the incident. Were either of you drinking?"

"Yes," Jacob mumbled.

"How much?"

"Just a couple beers. We were celebrating. It wasn't much."

"Tell us everything you remember about the accident?" Officer Nash asked.

"We couldn't sleep. We decided to ride our bikes out to the lake. Alex was in front of me when his bike slipped on a patch of ice. He slid into the road and was hit. I braked, hit the patch of ice and skidded too."

"Are you all right, Jacob?" Dale asked.

"Yes. The doctor said it was just some superficial scrapes."

"Consider yourself lucky," Officer Nash said.

"Can I see Alex now?"

"You have to wait for the doctor's okay," Dale explained.

Ava sat down on the other side of Jacob and wrapped her arm around him. Gwen stood up and followed the two officers out of the emergency room.

"What aren't you telling us?" she asked Liam. Liam looked at Officer Nash before responding. Nash nodded his okay then proceeded to the patrol car.

"It doesn't look good. The paramedics said Alex was unconscious when they found him, but still breathing. His right leg had been crushed. Jacob was found sitting on the ground not far from Alex, stunned, they said. They thought he might have a concussion as well. Fortunately another car was right behind the one that hit Alex. The driver called 911 so help arrived quickly. That's all we know so far."

"Thank you," Gwen told him. He tipped his hat then joined his partner.

Pastor Joe returned to the waiting room, leaving Alex's parents alone with him.

"How is he?" Dale asked.

"He's stable, but they need to do surgery on his legs."

"His legs?" Jacob asked.

"Yes. His right leg was crushed in the crash. They don't know whether they can save it. There's also damage to his left leg. He's lost a lot of blood."

"But if he loses his legs …" Jacob left the sentence hanging in the air.

"Yes. His days of playing basketball may be over."

Jacob shook his head, struggling to grasp what had been said.

"He may be in surgery for hours. We don't know when he'll be able to have visitors," Pastor Joe said. "There's nothing you can do here. You may as well go home."

"No. I'm not leaving. Not without seeing Alex," Jacob insisted.

Ava looked at Dale. "Someone should be home for Grace. What if she wakes up and no one is there?"

"I'll take you home, then come back and wait with Jacob," Dale said.

"You don't have to. I can make sure Jacob gets home safely." Gwen stepped forward.

"I don't know." Dale hesitated then looked at Pastor Joe. Pastor nodded in support of the suggestion. "Are you sure?" Dale looked from Jacob to Pastor Joe.

"He'll be fine," Pastor Joe assured him. "We'll take care of him."

Dale and Ava hugged Jacob and left. Alex's parents rejoined them in the waiting room.

"They're prepping Alex for surgery," Micah said as they sat down in the deserted waiting room.

Gwen pulled Pastor Joe aside.

"What do we do? Should we pray? Should I get some food and drinks?"

"Presence." Pastor Joe placed his hand on her shoulder. "Support them with your presence. Pray, yes, if that is what the family wants. But most of all, just be with them."

"How do I do that?" Gwen asked.

"Pray for guidance," Pastor Joe said then rejoined the three.

Guidance. Pray for guidance. What would that look like? Gwen looked back into the waiting room. She was needed there. She didn't have time for a long prayer.

"God, help me," she whispered, then rejoined the group.

It was two hours before the doctor came out to the waiting room. All five jumped up at her approach.

"He's stable," she said.

"His legs?" Micah asked.

"We were able to save the left one, but not the right. I'm sorry."

Alex's mother started crying. "But my boy is alive?"

"Yes, and expected to make a full recovery."

Alex's dad wrapped his arm around his wife. "When can we see him?

"He's in recovery now. Once he wakes up, you'll be able to see him, but just for a short time."

"Thank God," Taylor said, hugging her husband. "He's alive."

"But he won't be able to play basketball anymore," Jacob said.

"He's alive. That's all that matters."

Gwen waited with Jacob while Alex's parents went back and sat with him in recovery.

"Alex wants to see you," Alex's dad said to Jacob when they returned after twenty minutes.

"Do you want me to go with you?" Pastor Joe asked.

"No, that's all right, Pastor. Vicar Gwen can go with me if that's all right with her."

Gwen nodded her head and glanced at Pastor Joe before going back into recovery with Jacob.

"Bro," Alex said when he saw Jacob. They bumped fists. "What's up?"

"You. You're what's up," Jacob answered. Gwen waited at the foot of the bed.

"That was some game, wasn't it?"

"Sure was."

"And some celebration."

"You know it."

"Only now the doctors are saying something about my leg. I lost it?"

Jacob looked away from Alex, avoiding his gaze.

"Bro, you can tell me. What happened to my leg?"

Jacob looked at Gwen for help. Gwen stepped forward.

"That's right, Alex. They weren't able to save your leg."

"Rude. I guess I won't be getting my basketball scholarship after all."

"Don't say that," Jacob said. "We'll work out something. We're a team. I won't go anywhere that doesn't accept you."

"Naw, I wouldn't do that to you."

"Sure you can. All you have to do is get better. You let me worry about the rest."

"I guess." Alex's head bobbed as he fought sleep. "Whose idea was it? Riding to Otter Lake?"

"That would be you."

"Epic. I guess it wasn't as great an idea as I thought."

"Maybe not your best."

"I'll do better next time." Alex closed his eyes. "I'm sorry, bro."

"Sorry for what?"

"Putting you through this, ruining our big night."

"You just get better. That's all that matters."

"Maybe. If you say so." His breathing deepened.

"I think it's time we left." Gwen reached for Jacob, put her arm around him and led him out.

"It's my fault. All my fault. We never should have been drinking. Never should have snuck out. Why do I keep doing these things?" Jacob stopped her from going back into the waiting room.

Gwen waited. Presence, she told herself. Presence is enough. Like hell, she thought. God give me some words. She was surprised when Pastor Joe placed his hand on Jacob's shoulder. She hadn't seen him waiting for them outside of recovery.

"No one is assigning blame, Jacob, least of all Alex."

"Then he should."

"These things happen. You learn and move on."

"But I can move on with two legs. Alex only has one."

Pastor Joe hugged Jacob. He looked at Gwen. "Gwen. I think it's time you took Jacob home."

This time Jacob didn't resist the suggestion. Pastor Joe stayed with Alex's parents while Gwen took Jacob home, then went home herself to get ready for church.

Pastor Joe was already at church when she went over for the eleven o'clock service.

"Any more news?" Gwen asked.

"Nothing more than what you already know. Alex is stable."

"What about his parents?"

"You can ask them yourself. They're here. Said they needed their church community." Gwen was surprised to see Jacob in church as well, sitting with his family in their usual spot. She thought he would sleep in. That's what she would have done.

"Times like these, people realize their need for God and community. You okay?" Pastor Joe peered into her eyes.

"No, I'm not. But I guess that doesn't matter right now. I have a job to do."

"You do. Are you up to preaching?"

"I guess we'll both see."

Pastor Joe explained the events of the last night at the beginning of the service. At least she didn't have to be the one to break the news to the congregation. She just had to get through this service, then go home and collapse. Palm Sunday. How appropriate.

Gwen went to the pulpit after the reading of the Passion Narrative. The church was packed because of it being Palm Sunday, and, she suspected, because of the events of the previous night. Off to one side she thought she saw Officer Kelley, but not in his uniform. She took a deep breath and began.

"I thought I had my sermon ready Saturday morning, but then we had the state championship game and I came home and figured — how do I incorporate this into my sermon? Again, I thought I had my sermon done and went to bed only to be awakened at one o'clock and called to the hospital. Again, I needed to revise my sermon. That's life. It's seldom what you expect it to be. And I thought —

how like Palm Sunday. One hour you are celebrating. The next you are grieving. One day, crowds are cheering you and calling your name, the next you are gone.

"That's the fickleness of life. Through it all, one thing remains, our God's unfailing, steadfast love. God is crazy in love with us, his children, his creation, as fallible and fallen as we are. God loves us. God knows what it is to suffer all that we suffer in this life. He suffered it all himself. He became human, precisely so that we would have a God who knows what it is to be human. He came into this world as a man, Jesus.

"Alex wasn't alone in that operating room when the doctor removed his leg. Our God, Jesus, was with him. He was with Alex's parents in the waiting room and with his best friend, Jacob. God was with them, suffering along with them, because our God knows what it is to be human and suffer in this life." Gwen looked about the church, took a breath and proceeded.

"Some of you, maybe all of you, know about the Man of the Month Club." The congregation laughed at this. "My mom's attempt to find her daughter a man." Gwen pointed at her mom. "Yes, Mom, I'm talking about you." Her mom stood up and bowed to the congregation. "Well, I'm telling you, there is a man of the month, a man of the year, a man of the millennium. And that man is Jesus. He chose to suffer and die for us. He chose to humble himself, become human, so that we would have a God who knows what it is to be human. So we would have a God we can relate to. In all of life's challenges and struggles, all of life's losses, we know, our God understands what it is to suffer in this life. He died for all of us here. He died for Alex so that Alex in his pain would know he is not alone. And neither are any of us."

Gwen was embarrassed to see Liam amongst the church members staying for coffee and donuts after the service.

"Since when have you been a member?" she asked.

"There are times when a man needs a church community, especially when he sees so much of the darker side of life."

"Angie didn't come with you?"

"No, she doesn't get up on the weekends until noon. I came alone." He offered Gwen a cup of coffee. "What you said today. It was great. Thank you. I needed to hear that."

"Thank you," Gwen responded. Now if only she believed it herself.

Chapter 42

Gwen plopped herself down in her usual seat for her weekly meeting with Pastor Joe. "I'm done."

"Holy Week. Always happens during Holy Week."

"What are you talking about?"

"This far through the internship, I often get told that."

"I'm serious. I am done. I'm not cut out to be a pastor. I can't do what you do."

"By the way, your sermon last Sunday. Nicely done."

A number of people had told her that. It didn't make a difference. She knew she wasn't up to being a pastor.

"I can't do this. It's too hard. I'm hardly adequate for the task."

"Sometimes it's not a matter of being adequate. God fills our inadequacies."

"Even God can't fill all of my failings. I can't handle it. All those suffering people, the deaths. I can't do it. You said yourself that this year is to help determine whether ordination is the right path for me. That if someone decides they aren't cut out or fit, then you've done your job."

"That's assuming they truly aren't cut out for the pastorate. But if they are running away from a true call from God, and I let them, then I have failed."

"Is it running away, or recognizing your limits?"

"That's for you to tell me."

"All I know is that I can't do this anymore. It hurts too much. Besides, I'm a failure. I've failed Jacob and Alex. And I've failed you. It's my fault, what happened Saturday night."

"Funny how people want to claim blame for something they had nothing to do with."

"Because I knew Jacob and Alex were drinking, but I didn't tell anyone."

"On the night of the accident?"

"No, back in September, at the picnic. They had alcohol in their 'water' thermoses. I knew it had been dumped out but I didn't tell their parents. I wanted to be the trendy minister. One they could trust."

"And that's why you aren't cut out to be a pastor?"

"If I had told their parents, they would have watched them more carefully, put a stop to their drinking."

"That's easier said than done," Pastor Joe commented. "Perhaps it was a lapse in judgment, not telling on them. You are their minister, not their friend. But there's no guarantee that, if Alex and Jacob's parents had known, they would have been able to prevent them from sneaking out and drinking. I ought to know. My Stephanie was no saint in high school."

"But at least it wouldn't have been my fault."

"You can beat yourself up about this, or you can do whatever is in your power to make amends."

"How?"

"By apologizing to Alex and Jacob's parents, and to the boys too. Admitting your mistakes and then sticking by them. Helping them get through this rather than backing out now when they need you. Alex has a long way to go. He hasn't begun to realize the extent of his loss. And Jacob needs help too. He'll need help forgiving himself for what happened to his best friend."

"What if I'm not the right person to help?"

"Whether you are or not, you're the one God has placed in their lives at this particular junction."

"You're saying I can't just give up and go home."

"Yes. Besides, Cascade Falls is your home."

"You know what I mean."

"I know that this is a learning year for you. Complete your internship and, if you still feel you aren't cut out for ordination, I'll back you up in your decision."

"Even if it means the seminary won't send you any more interns?"

"We are a long way from that happening. You let me worry about that." Gwen nodded her head and stood up. "Oh, and remember, we've got the rest of Holy Week to get through and Easter Sunday. These crises seem to have a way of happening during Holy Week, the busiest time of the year for a pastor. Remember that when you're a pastor."

"If I'm ever a pastor." Gwen shook her head and left.

It had not been the outcome she was looking for. She wanted to give this up and escape back to her exciting and yet safe existence as a student in Chicago.

She was trapped once again in Cascade Falls. At least until the end of her internship year. Just like she had been most of her life.

Chapter 43

Easter Sunday came and went but there was no resurrection within her. At least she didn't have to preach.

Gwen had spoken to both Alex's parents and Jacob's parents.

"You're telling me this now?" Alex's mother had exploded. "Now when our baby is lying in a hospital bed recovering from a tragic accident that could have been prevented? You're not fit to be a minister."

Gwen actually preferred her reaction to the understanding she received from Dale and Ava. She deserved condemnation, not forgiveness.

"We would have appreciated knowing about this, but you wouldn't have been telling us anything we didn't already know, or at least suspected. Teens often experiment with drinking. We both know that. Jacob is certainly no saint. We know that as well. We were hoping if we didn't make a big deal out of it, it would just be a passing phase," Dale told her.

"You can't keep your kids safe all the time. Sometimes despite your best efforts, they do things, take chances you don't approve of. We couldn't keep him locked up inside his room," Ava added.

"Or, we could have tried locking him in his room, but we would have had to let him out sometime." Dale smiled. It didn't make her feel better.

When Gwen apologized to Alex and Jacob, they were both surprised. She talked to them in Alex's hospital room.

"Telling our parents wouldn't have made any difference," Jacob told her.

"Yeah. We would have continued drinking, but then we wouldn't have trusted you," Alex said.

"You didn't tell us to sneak off on our bikes and drink. We did that ourselves. And we have to live with the consequences," Jacob added.

"I have to bro. Last I noticed, you still had two legs and a basketball scholarship."

"And you won't let me forget it, will you?"

"You're right there," Alex said. "You owe me. You are never going to live this down."

"Nor do I want to." There was a seriousness behind their teasing banter that Gwen couldn't miss. She still felt she was to blame. How could she make it up to them? How could she forgive herself?

Chapter 44

The spring sun shone bright as small children ran about the school grounds, rushing from booth to booth, followed by parents, grandparents, and older siblings. For Earth Day, the HOPE Club, comprised mostly of the youth group, was doing an environment fair at the high school. Under the direction of Josie and Grace, they had set up booths outside with information on global warming, recycling, the dangers of plastics, the importance of preserving the rain forests, and ways to cut back on your carbon footprint. Each booth had handouts with information on the danger posed by the different threats to the environment and what can be done to help. The local power company had a booth with information on conserving energy and energy alternatives. Josie and Grace were at the registration table. Everyone who attended was given an ecofriendly bag and a small fir tree to plant along with information about the benefit of trees for the ecosystem.

Jacob and Alex were at a booth with a small basketball hoop and ball for kids. Alex was in a wheelchair. He needed to regain his strength and for his leg to be fully healed before he could be fitted for a prosthesis. Thanks to his youth and his athletic ability, he was healing quicker than his doctor had originally thought. His parents still refused to talk to Gwen or even acknowledge her presence. They hovered over their son as if by doing so they could turn back time to when their son could walk. Gwen longed for that time to. She went over to their booth to see if they needed anything.

"What does this have to do with the environment?" Pastor Joe walked over to their booth. He was attending with his wife Kathleen and their two-year-old grandson, Gus.

"Spin the wheel and get a question on the environment. If you get the question right you get a chance for a free throw to win a prize. The answers to each question can be found at the different booths. If you don't know the answer, you can go to that booth then come back and try again," Jacob explained.

Pastor Joe spun the wheel and ended at the category for global warming.

"How many acres of rain forest are we losing each year?" Alex read.

Pastor Joe looked at Kathleen. "I guess I'm not as up on this as I thought. Maybe I better go to the booth on global warming."

"You do that. Hey little bro," Alex wheeled over to Gus. "You want a free throw? I'll help you." Alex put Gus in his lap and gave him the ball, then rolled close enough to the hoop for Gus to drop it in. Jacob gave him a piece of candy, which the two-year-old quickly unwrapped and popped in his mouth. When more candy wasn't forthcoming, he wriggled out of Alex's lap and ran to another booth. Kathleen took off running after him.

"Got to start early to recruit basketball players," Alex told Pastor Joe.

Gwen went back to the registration table to give Josie a break. Officer Kelley sauntered over.

"You did a great job organizing this," he said as he surveyed the turnout. Gwen estimated two to three hundred people were there. Not bad for their first attempt.

"Josie and Grace get the credit. It was their idea. They did most of the work. I just provided support.

"Then you did a great job supporting them."

"At least I'm good for something."

"I would think you are good for more than that."

Gwen's mother joined them, holding onto Sam's leash.

"Mom, why did you bring Sam?"

"He needs the fresh air and exercise. Besides, the children love him." Laura turned to Liam, struggling to hold Sam. "Officer Kelley, are you flirting with my daughter?" Gwen kicked her mother in the shin.

"Why it's you I'm really after," Liam winked at Laura.

"I'm not available. My daughter, however —"

"Mom. Stop it."

Officer Kelley smiled, tipped his hat and excused himself.

"Mom, you've got to stop doing that."

"Doing what? Loving my daughter? Looking out for her best interests?" When Gwen didn't respond, her mother gave her Sam's leash. "Here, take care of your dog."

"I'm not the one who brought him out here. Don't you see I'm working here?"

"And I'm working too, on your behalf. That dog is your man magnet."

A squirrel appeared on the other side of the fair. Sam jumped up from Gwen's feet and took off running, knocking over people, chairs and whole booths in his way, dragging his leash behind him. Gwen ran after him, bumping into the people, chairs and booths he had knocked over.

Officer Kelley reached Sam before she did. He was scratching Sam about his ears by the time she arrived. Breathless, Gwen thanked him.

"This is getting to be a habit," Liam smiled as he handed her Sam's leash.

"I'm sorry," Gwen said, then looked back at the path of destruction behind her. Liam looked too.

"Maybe I should take Sam back to your house."

"That would help. I'm so sorry to bother you with this."

"No bother at all."

Gwen took a deep breath. Where to begin? Pastor Joe and the youth group were picking up the knocked over people, chairs, and booths. Gus was laughing and running through the crowd. Jacob and Alex already had their booth up and running again. Josie was struggling to get up after being knocked down. Jacob rushed over and helped her up then helped her and Grace set up the registration table again.

"No harm, no foul," Jacob said when she approached.

"Why can't you control that dog?" Mrs. Wickersham snapped at her. "He's a menace. Pastor, what are you going to do about this? We can't have that dog living in our rectory. God only knows what he is doing to the furniture."

"Yes, Mrs. Wickersham, God only knows," Pastor Joe responded. "You kids okay?"

"A little bruised," Grace said. Josie sat down.

"Josie, you okay?"

"I'm fine, Pastor. I'm just a little sore." Josie cringed as she tried to hide the pain she was feeling.

"You don't look okay. We better call your parents."

"Please don't. You know how they worry."

"Because they love you. We better take you to the emergency room to get checked out, just in case." Pastor Joe pulled his cell phone out of his pocket.

"I have to help clean up," Josie insisted.

"Don't worry, Josie. Alex and I will make sure everything's taken care of. You go ahead and leave," Jacob insisted.

"Are you sure?"

"Since when am I not sure?"

Josie didn't answer as she winced again.

"Can I come with Josie?" Grace asked.

"Sure, Grace," Gwen said. "I'll finish up here." She turned to Josie. "I'm so sorry, Josie."

"It's okay. I fall easily. It's not Sam's fault," Josie said as Pastor Joe led her away.

"Sometimes it seems trouble follows you." Gwen was not happy to hear this familiar voice. Adelle. Adelle didn't wait for a response. "See you Thursday," she said as she walked away.

Yes. Trouble does follow her.

Chapter 45

Despite her complaints, Pastor Joe continued to insist she keep her monthly appointments for spiritual direction. She definitely would not miss meeting with Adelle once she got back to Chicago.

"What did you learn?" he would ask after each session.

"Nothing. When can I stop wasting my time?"

"When you stop wasting your time and start to learn," Pastor Joe would respond.

What would Adelle say and do this time? With the spring weather, Gwen was ushered outside and given a hoe.

"Time to start preparing the soil for another season."

Gwen knew better than to complain. Complaints would result in no sympathy and perhaps a clod of soil thrown at her.

"I love this time of preparation. Digging in the dirt, getting it ready to plant seeds or the plants I've been growing inside. It's a wonderful time of year."

"You say that about every season." Gwen leaned on the hoe.

"Do I now? Maybe because it's true. Whatever season of life you are in, it's a great season."

"If you say so."

"I know so. Look at you. You're in the spring of your life. You are still just getting ready, preparing the soil, pulling the weeds, digging out rocks. Eventually you'll be ready for planting. Some soil takes longer than others to prep. There are rocks and thorns that need to be pulled. But you'll be ready. Eventually."

"And if I'm not? What if I'm never ready? What if I'm not cut out for ministry?"

"Oh no. You're cut out for it. You've got the gift. You just don't know it yet."

"What if I don't want the gift?"

"It can't be refused. You already have it. It can be ignored, but at your own peril."

"What do you mean my own peril?"

"God gives us gifts to use. If we don't use them, they wither up inside us, leaving us a hollow shell."

"And if I do use them?"

"Then you will receive fruit in abundance, blessings overflowing." Adelle cupped her hands, dug into the soil and allowed it to flow between her fingers.

"I don't see any fruit for all my efforts." Gwen frowned and pushed the hoe into the soil, then reached down and picked out a rock.

"That's because you need more fertilizer."

"You mean more shit?" Gwen grimaced.

"Isn't that life? Shit happens. That's the fertilizer for growth." Adelle lifted a clump of dirt, smelled it and held it out to Gwen. "Hmmm. God's good soil. Doesn't get much better than that."

Gwen chose to ignore the comment and focused on her hoeing, remaining silent until it was time to leave lest Adelle say more she didn't want to hear.

Chapter 46

What a relief. Josie hadn't been hurt by the fall. At least Gwen wouldn't have that on her conscience along with all she was already carrying around. Josie was bruised but suffered no broken bones. Still Gwen apologized profusely at the next HOPE club meeting.

"I'm so sorry about Sam messing everything up."

"Sam didn't know any better. He's just a dog," Grace spoke in defense of the mastiff.

"I know. But he's my dog. I'm responsible for him."

"Don't worry, Vicar Gwen. You can make it up to us by buying us ice cream," Jacob said.

"That I can do," Gwen responded. If only all of life's problems were so easily solved.

Grace and Josie were the last two people she wanted to let down. She felt like she had let everyone else down. She hadn't done any of the great things she had envisioned when the year started. She never did get around to starting that vlog, and the drama team she had started with such hope had fizzled after three productions. Not that they weren't well received. She just didn't have the time and energy to keep it going and hadn't found anyone to take it on for her. The people she had been assigned to visit had all died, one by one. She was beginning to feel like the angel of death. The young adult group was going on just fine without any effort on her part. The only thing she had to show for the year was the youth group and HOPE club and she had messed that up too.

She had failed miserably. Was this the "shit" Adelle was talking about? If so, she didn't see how any of it was going to bear fruit. She was plodding along, waiting for the end of the year so she could go back to Chicago and quit. Find something else to do with her life.

"Are you still considering quitting ministry?" Pastor Joe asked.

"I promised you I would complete the year, but nothing has happened to change my mind. If anything, it has just strengthened my resolve to quit."

"What are you going to do?"

"I could change majors. Get a degree in liturgical studies rather than seeking ordination. Then I could plan liturgies, form drama teams, use my background in drama to serve God."

"Or?" Pastor Joe waited for her to continue.

"Or, maybe I could join Second City in Chicago. I completed their course on Improv. They told me to come back and audition whenever I was ready. I could serve God by making people laugh."

"That you could. But you could also serve as a pastor by making people laugh. We all need laughter in our life."

"I think I've angered more people than I've made laugh."

"That is part of being a pastor too. Do you think everyone liked what Jesus said and did?"

"No, of course not. Or they wouldn't have killed him."

"Look, you have one more month before you go back to seminary."

"If I haven't changed my mind by now, do you really think one month will make a difference?"

"You'd be surprised what can happen in a month, especially in God's time."

"Then it's up to God to make it happen," Gwen said as she was leaving.

Chapter 47

After dating for seven years, Chloe, the director of Joy's School of Dance, was finally getting married to Officer Nash. Many at the church had said it would never happen. Others had insisted it was inevitable. And now, the inevitable was happening.

Gwen knew Chloe from her involvement with the dance studio her senior year in college. Since coming back, she had been too busy at the church to spend much time reconnecting with her friends there. Still, as the intern, she was helping out with the service and had been invited to the reception.

Since Chloe was Catholic and Officer Nash, Lutheran, it was to be an ecumenical service with Fr. John and Pastor Joe co-officiating. The service was to be held in the gardens outside of St. Luke's, with the reception following in the church hall.

Kathleen, Pastor Joe's wife, along with Chloe's friend Sara were bridesmaids. Chloe's friend Letty was maid of honor. Liam was Officer Nash's best man. All of the local police force was going to be there in their dress blues, as well as all of the teachers, parents and students from the dance studio. Chloe's daughter Mary was the flower girl; Officer Nash's nephew Clay, the ring bearer. Sara's nine-year-old twins Gabriel and Angela were in charge of the guest book. It was to be the event of the year for the town of Cascade Falls. How could she miss it?

Gwen had invited Matthew as her date.

"I thought the Man of the Month Club was over since you 'outed' it on Palm Sunday. You no longer need a decoy to save you from embarrassing first dates."

"It is, but I still need a date. I need someone to dance with at the reception. It will be fun." Gwen had managed to convince him.

Her only responsibility was to help with the music until Kathleen approached her, pushing Gus in his stroller

"Stephanie got called into work. I didn't have time to get a babysitter. Would you watch Gus for me? Just during the service?"

How hard would it be to watch a two-year-old? "Sure," Gwen agreed.

"Great. Here's his diaper bag. There's a box of raisins in the side pouch if he gets too restless. No candy. He goes berserk when he eats chocolate."

Gwen swung the backpack onto her shoulder. So much for the classy ensemble she had put together for the wedding. She pushed Gus in his stroller while people started arriving for the service. When Gus got restless, she let him out of the stroller to stretch his legs. Mistake. Gus took off for the chairs and started running up and down the aisle and through the wedding archway. When Gwen caught up to him and picked him up, he started screaming. Gwen reached into the backpack for the raisins and gave the box to Gus. Gus opened the box and began to meticulously take one out at a time, popping the fruit into his mouth, then diving back in for another. She sat down in the last row of chairs and set Gus into his stroller, forgetting to strap him in.

"Hey, 'Lil bro." Alex rolled up alongside Gus' stroller. "What's up?"

Jacob sat down next to Gwen. "How did you end up babysitting Gus?" he asked. "Wait, don't tell me. Stephanie was a no-show."

"You might say that." Gwen saw some commotion among the members of the praise team. "Could you watch him for a minute?"

"Sure. We're buddies, aren't we, Gus?" Alex tried to fist-bump the hand that held the box of raisins. Gus ignored him.

By the time Gwen made it to the praise team, whatever problem they had had been resolved.

"Enjoy the wedding," the praise leader told her.

Gwen went back to her seat as Alex handed Gus a piece of chocolate. Gus had the chocolate unwrapped and in his mouth before Gwen could grab it out of his fingers.

"He's not supposed to have chocolate."

"It was only two pieces," Alex said. "What could that hurt?"

"Two pieces," Gwen repeated. Yikes. "Maybe it will be okay." Please, God, let it be okay, she prayed.

The wedding music started. Pastor Joe and Fr. John stood in front of the flower covered arch that had been brought in for the service. The groom and groomsmen lined up on the side. Gus started squirming in his stroller. When Kathleen started down the aisle, Gus shouted, "Gamma," and jumped out of the stroller before Gwen could stop him. He ran down the side row of chairs. Gwen followed after him, slouching down, trying not to be seen or to disrupt the service. She snuck up behind him and picked him up. Gus screamed then sunk his teeth into Gwen's shoulder. Gwen continued to hold onto him till he bit her finger and drew blood.

Gwen bit down to keep from screaming herself, letting Gus go as she held her hand and her tongue. Pain shot up her arm. Gus ran up to the wedding arch, pulling on the lacey canopy as he ran in and out of the archway, causing the arch to sway. Pastor Joe passed his book to Fr. John and ran after his grandson, scooping him up as the archway started to tumble towards the bride and groom. Liam made a quick save, catching the structure before it landed on the bridal party then holding it up till, with the help of the other groomsmen, they were able to secure the archway back into its assigned spot. The congregation watched in horror until Pastor Joe turned with Gus and smiled.

"This will be a story to tell your grandchildren," he told the bride and groom. He then looked for Gwen who was standing off to the side, holding her hand. The wound was a mere surface scratch and had stopped bleeding with pressure.

"I'm okay," Gwen let go of her bloodied hand and showed it to the congregation. "Just a flesh wound."

Pastor Joe brought Gus to her. "Chocolate," he shook his head as he placed Gus into her arms. The tell-tale sign of chocolate was around Gus' mouth.

Gwen carried Gus back to his stroller, this time making sure to securely strap him in. Then she pushed the stroller across the parking lot to the school playground where Gus could run without disturbing the wedding any further.

Matthew found her there.

"Sorry I'm late," he said. "At least I made it in time for the reception." Matthew looked about at the full parking lot. "Why are you here and not at the ceremony?"

"Gus," Gwen pointed at him then showed him her finger. "The little monster bit me, twice. He knocked down the wedding archway, all on my watch." Gus was playing in the sand, scooping up buckets of sand and pouring it on some trucks.

"That little angel?" Matthew smiled over at Gus.

"You try watching him."

"I'll do that. You better put something on your finger."

"It'll be okay."

"No, the human mouth is full of germs. Put some antiseptic on it. Go on."

Gwen went into the church office, found the first aid kit, poured hydrogen peroxide on her wound, squeezing it first to open the wound so the peroxide could work its magic. She watched the peroxide bubble to show it was doing its job. She couldn't find any Band-Aids so ended up wrapping her finger with gauze, creating a bulging bandage on her finger. She frowned. The perfect complement to her ensemble.

When she came back to the playground the service was over. Jacob and Alex had joined Matthew.

"Best wedding ever," Jacob said. "At least the beginning. After that it was boring."

"Yeah. 'Lil bro sure knows how to liven up a party," Alex said.

"You had to give him chocolate," Gwen said. "He almost ruined the wedding."

"If you ask me, I think he saved it. Who wants a boring, picture-perfect wedding anyway," Jacob said.

"The bride," Gwen responded.

"Chloe will be okay with it. After all those years running recitals, she knows about runaway toddlers stealing the show," Jacob assured her.

They stayed at the playground as guests drifted out of the service and into the church hall.

"When does the social hour begin?" Jacob asked.

"Never for you," Gwen reminded him.

"Hey, we learned our lesson. Nothing stronger than apple cider until we're legal," he told her. "Right Alex?"

Alex nodded his agreement.

When pictures were done, Kathleen came in search of Gus.

"You were a hit," she told him as she picked him up and put him in his stroller. "I can take it from here. My duties are over for now. Come on, Gus. Grandma's going to get a glass of wine, then we are going into the ladies' room where you can play."

Gwen gave a sigh of relief as they left.

"Come on, Gwen. You could use a glass of wine too," Matthew said.

"A glass or two," Gwen commented as she watched the wedding party proceed to the church hall. Angie walked beside Liam, hanging onto his arm and laughing. Matthew glanced at Gwen then back at the couple, following Gwen's gaze.

"Or more. Come on, girlfriend. We're going to have a good time tonight. Leave it to me." Matthew took her arm and escorted her inside.

Chapter 48

Applause erupted and glasses clinked after the traditional toasts by the maid of honor and best man. Then the floor was opened for anyone else who wanted to share a toast. Kathleen raised her glass and reminded Chloe about how she had showed up in Cascade Falls to stay with her grandfather seven years ago.

"You showed up on our doorstop, pregnant and in need of a job and we couldn't be happier. You are part of our family now."

Pastor Joe talked about Chloe's grandfather, Howard, reminding her of how much he loved her and was proud of her. Then the groomsmen, all cops, ribbed Officer Nash with stories from their years on the force together. As Fr. John prepared to give the blessing, Liam's girlfriend stood up, glass in hand.

"This is such a wonderful occasion. I can't think of any better time to announce our engagement than here." Liam tried to pull her down. When there was no response from those gathered, Angie continued. "That's right. The best man, Officer Liam Kelley and I are getting married and I can assure you, he is the best man, if you know what I mean." There was a shallow round of applause and congratulations. Liam succeeded in getting her to sit down as Fr. John began the blessing over the meal.

"Can this day get any worse?" Gwen gulped down her glass of wine.

"Let me get you another glass of wine." Matthew stood up then whispered, "I'll take care of that—" The word was lost amidst the clinking of silverware against glasses as the wedding guests demanded another kiss from the bride and groom, followed by applause.

"I just want to get this dinner over with so I can slip out as soon as socially acceptable," Gwen replied.

"Not without a dance. You promised me there would be dancing."

"That's right, Gwen. You can't leave before the dance," Leon said. Gwen was seated at a table with other young adults, including Leon, Roger and Gordon and their dates. "I'll save a dance for you." His date gave him a kick under the table. "Just one dance, sweetie. Can't you see she's lonely."

"I'm fine, Leon," Gwen looked around for her date. "Matthew, where's that drink?"

After dinner, Gwen saw Kathleen disappear into the ladies' room again with Gus. That's where she found her when it was time for the bridal party to dance.

"Kathleen, they're looking for you. Time for your dance." Gus was playing with cars, climbing from chair to chair along the counter in front of the mirrors that lined the lounge area of the restroom. "I can watch Gus."

"That's okay." Kathleen finished her wine then gathered Gus' cars. "Gus can dance with me. Can't you, buddy? Your grandpa can help." She packed Gus' cars in his backpack then reached for Gus. "Stephanie gets off work soon, then she'll take him home for bedtime. Isn't that right, Gus?"

At the word "bed," Gus said no and ran into the room with the stalls and headed under them. Kathleen and Gwen chased after him as he crawled from stall to stall.

"Gus, come out of there. Grandma can't crawl in this dress."

Kathleen went into the open stall on one end and Gwen went to the other end. There was a scream out of one of the occupied stalls, then a laugh out of the other, till Gus made it to Gwen's stall. Gwen scooped him up before he had a chance to turn around and crawl back the other way.

"He'll be the death of me yet," Kathleen said as Gwen handed him back to her. "But he's also my life," she added as she hugged him. "Let's see if your mom is here yet."

As Kathleen left, Gwen was almost run over by Angie.

"You," she said when she saw Gwen. "It's all your fault."

"What's my fault?"

"That date of yours." There was a large red stain down the front of her orchid dress.

Gwen fought back the laughter that threatened to choke her. "I'm so sorry," she managed to get out, then rushed out of the bathroom and burst into laughter.

"I told you I'd take care of her," Matthew said when she came back to her table just as the bridal party finished their dance. "Now's your chance. Go on, dance with your officer."

"But I …" Gwen started then took a gulp of wine and went out on the dance floor.

"Care to dance?" Gwen held out her hand. Liam looked around for his date. "She's temporarily indisposed. Shall we?"

Liam smiled and put his arm around her and swung her as the DJ played "I Wanna Dance with Somebody." Pastor Joe joined Kathleen and Gus on the dance floor. Gwen laughed as she looked around the floor. She was surrounded by friends. Leon and the gang from her table, church members, youth group members. Matthew came up and danced with Gus, freeing Pastor Joe to dance with Kathleen. Alex was whirling about in his wheelchair. Maybe Cascade Falls wasn't so bad. She laughed at Liam as he swirled her under his arm and out again. Maybe she would miss this place after all when she left.

"What are you smiling about?" Liam asked.

"I'm thinking I'm going to miss this place when I leave. It's been an okay year after all."

"Just this place?"

"No, the people. The people make the place. It's been more than okay."

Gwen swung into Liam's arm again, only to feel someone grab her and pull her away. Angie was out of the restroom, her front wet and still stained from the red wine.

"Stay away from my fiancé." Angie pulled her arm back and prepared to slug Gwen. Liam stopped her then pulled her off the dance floor.

Without missing a beat, Matthew stepped in and swept her away. Gwen watched as Liam left the hall with Angie.

"Remember, we're here to have fun. Don't worry about them," Matthew yelled into her ear above the music.

"I know," Gwen said. "But I think I'll sit the next one out." Gwen sat down by herself at her table. The table seemed to be swirling. All that wine. Maybe now would be a good time to sneak out and go home. She could always use Sam as an excuse. Say she had to walk him.

She saw Liam and Angie come back in from wherever they had gone. Angie grabbed her clutch purse from where she had left it at their table then held onto Liam's arm as they went out the front door.

Yes, this would be a good time to get some fresh air. She slipped out and went over to the church garden, scene of the soon-to-be infamous wedding arch incident. She imagined people would be telling that story long after she was gone. It had been posted on YouTube and was getting thousands of likes. At two, Gus was already more famous than she would ever be. The archway had been removed. Chairs were being stacked and put away by the rental company. Soon all evidence that there had been a wedding here would be gone. Soon she would be gone too and her year here but a memory. A mixed memory.

She sat down on a concrete seat in the garden and stared about her. The sun was emitting its last rays of red in a farewell to the day. Gwen shivered as a breeze kicked up.

"Cold?" a voice asked. Without waiting for a response, a jacket was placed on her bare shoulders. Liam.

"I thought you left."

"I can't leave. I'm part of the bridal party. I have to stay till the bitter end. I just escorted Angie to her car. She went home."

"I know. Her dress was ruined. Sorry about that."

"You seem to apologize all the time for things you are not responsible for."

"Well, maybe I am. My date spilled his drink on her on purpose."

"That was your date, not you."

"He did it for me, so I could dance with you."

"Oh. He succeeded."

"Yes, he did." They sat in silence for a while. Gwen looked down at the gauze bandage on her finger and started to pick at it.

"I meant to ask you about that. Gus?"

"Yes. He's got quite the bite."

"You should have that looked at."

"I know."

"The human mouth is full of germs," they said in unison then laughed.

"You know," Liam began, "I remember you from that afternoon years ago. I was a rookie cop. You were so daring, standing up to those traffickers, swinging that bat. I think I was in love with you from that moment."

"Wait. What are you saying?"

"And then, that Christmas Eve when you came to the hospital with your mother. I thought you were courageous then. But never braver than that night when Alex lost his leg. How you stayed with Jacob throughout the night and then your message on Palm Sunday."

"What are you saying, Officer Kelley? Aren't you engaged?"

"And aren't you dating Matthew?"

They both paused then said at the same time. "He's gay" and "We broke up."

"You did?" and "I know." Said again at the same time. They laughed.

"Okay," Liam said. "How about you go first."

"Sounds like a good idea. You know what?"

"I know that Matthew is gay."

"And you broke up? I thought Angie just announced to the world ..."

Liam put his finger on her lips to quiet her. "We were never engaged. That was more Angie's wishful thinking than reality. I guess I went along with it because it was easier that way. Until ..."

"Until what?"

"Until I could no longer take the easy way. How could I be engaged to one woman when I thought I might be in love with someone else?"

"Someone else?" Gwen leaned forward. Liam lifted her chin with his hand.

"You. You marvelous mixture of grace and mishap. Wherever you go, adventure follows. And I'm not saying this because of the Thunderbird." Liam leaned in to kiss her as Gwen pulled back.

"The Thunderbird? You know about the Thunderbird?"

"Sure, doesn't everybody? It's all part of the Man of the Month Club. Whoever finds a man for you gets your mom's Thunderbird."

"No, I never told anyone about the Thunderbird. How did you know?"

Liam pulled back, as if carefully considering his words. "Your mother."

"My mother? What about my mother?" The warm feeling dissipated at the mention of her mother. Now what had her mother done?

"Your mother. She approached me about dating you months ago, back in the summer. She told me about the Man of the Month Club, even offered me her Thunderbird if I could get you to like me."

"So that's what this is all about? All my mother's doing? Part of her plot to keep me in Cascade Falls? You get me to like you and you get the Thunderbird? How dare you."

"No, it's not like that at all. I told her no. Besides, I was dating Angie at the time. That didn't seem to matter to your mother."

"No, insignificant details like a girlfriend never seem to matter to my mother." Gwen stood up. "So, it's all been a sham. From that very first night at the Crab Shack?"

"No. It's not a sham. I knew about your mother's plan, but I wasn't part of it. You have to believe me." Liam stood up and took her hand.

"Then how come you were there at the Crab Shack? How come you keep showing up?"

"I was intrigued. Couldn't help it. I wondered, what mother would offer a Thunderbird to get her daughter a date? Not a lot happens here in Cascade Falls. It can be pretty boring. And then I saw you and remembered you from years ago. Then, those clowns trying to pick you up. I don't know. I had always thought fate would bring us together some time. It seemed like fate kept bringing us together."

"My mother didn't have anything to do with it?"

"No."

"Or the Thunderbird?"

"Hey, it looks like a sweet ride, that did intrigue me, but no. Then I got to know you. This is all about you, you crazy, wonderful, woman."

"How can I believe you? I'll never know whether this is about me or my mom's twisted plot."

"What if your mom's plot brought us together? What's wrong with that?"

"Everything. And if you can't understand that, then clearly you don't know me as well as you think you do." Gwen pulled her hand away from his.

"Then give me a chance to get to know you better." Liam reached for her hand.

"No, I'll never know whether you are interested in me or the Thunderbird." Gwen turned around and left. She returned to the reception long enough to let Matthew know she was leaving.

Her mom stopped her before she left. "Where are you going? I saw you dancing with Officer Kelley. You make a great couple."

"Really? Really, Mom. What do you know about it?"

"Nothing. I was just saying—"

"You've done enough, Mom. You and your club. Well, all your schemes have backfired. You've ruined my life. Just leave me alone, let me get through this month and then I'll be gone for good. And when I'm gone, I'm never coming back to Cascade Falls."

She went home to Sam. She was glad for his company, even though he had been part of another one of her mom's schemes. It wasn't his fault any more than it was her fault.

Chapter 49

Laura watched her daughter leave the reception.

"What was that all about?" Margie asked. Laura had gone over to the table were her friends were sitting with their husbands. She saw Officer Kelley enter by a side door and sit at a table in the back by himself.

"I don't know, but I'm going to find out." She walked over to the bar and ordered a whiskey. "Make that a double," she said then went back to where Liam was seated.

"Buy you a drink?" She sat down and set the drink on the table in front of Liam.

"You just ruined my life."

"Why do people keep saying that?"

"Maybe because it's true."

"How did I ruin your life?"

"You and your Man of the Month club. You just lost me the love of my life."

"Really? Gwen, you are talking about my Gwen, aren't you?" Laura reached for the whiskey and took a sip.

"Yes, your daughter, but now, thanks to you, she won't talk to me."

"You have to talk to her."

"It won't do any good. She insists that you and your meddling have ruined her life and now it has ruined mine." Liam reached for the whiskey.

"How? What did I do this time?"

"I told her how you had approached me about Man of the Month Club last summer."

"But you turned me down, though you were interested in my Thunderbird."

"Sweet ride." Both nodded their heads in agreement on this. "But that doesn't matter. It doesn't matter that I turned you down. She doesn't believe me. Nothing matters anymore." Liam took a swallow of whiskey then passed it back to Laura.

"What possessed you to tell her?"

"I don't know. I didn't want to start our relationship on a lie. That's no way to form a solid relationship." He stared down at the table.

"How little you know about relationships." Laura took another sip of the whiskey. "So now she refuses to talk to you?"

"She says you've been meddling in her life all these years."

"I'm a mother. It's what I do."

"Now wait a minute." Liam looked up at her. "The dog, Sam. You knew I loved that dog."

"How could I know that?" Laura took another sip, looking at him from over the rim of the glass.

"At the station. Sam was at the police station before he was taken to the shelter. I remember, you were in there for something, some form. Or was that just an excuse?"

"Go on," Laura continued to sip, hiding behind the glass.

"Anyway. Sam was at my desk, sitting beside me. That's how you knew. You arranged for Gwen to get that dog knowing I would somehow help with him."

"And if I did?"

"And you let him out that night so I'd come looking for Gwen."

"A mother's got to do what a mother's got to do."

"Gwen was right. You have been behind this all along, Only I didn't see it."

"All I did was help you two get together. What's so wrong with that? The rest you did yourself." She continued to sip whiskey.

"No wonder Gwen was upset."

"Look, do you love my daughter?" Laura sat the whiskey down and looked directly at Liam.

"Yes."

"Do you want her back?"

"Of course."

"That's all I need to know. You let me take care of the rest. I made this mess. I'll clean it up."

"How? She won't talk to either of us."

"She can refuse to talk to you, but she can't refuse to talk to me forever. I am her mother after all." Laura finished off the whiskey then stood up. "I'll be in touch," she told him as she walked back to her table, holding onto the tops of chairs as she went.

Chapter 50

Someone was poking her. Was it a nightmare? She really did have too much to drink last night.

"Get up."

Gwen opened her eyes and saw her mother. This was a nightmare, a real-life nightmare. She rolled over. "Go away."

"I'm not going anywhere till you get up."

"I'm not talking to you," Gwen mumbled. "How did you get in here anyway?"

"Remember. Church secretary. I'm the keeper of the keys." Laura dangled her keys in front of Gwen. "Even if you won't talk to me, you will talk to your dad, won't you?"

"Sure."

"Good, because he's here" Laura stepped back and her dad stepped forward. "I'll be downstairs making French toast. Don't take too long. Besides you have to get up for church anyway."

"I'm not going to church. I'm not going anywhere you'll be." Gwen shouted at her mother as she left. "Hi, Daddy." She sat up in bed. "What are you doing here?"

"Your mother said if I wanted breakfast, I had to come with her and talk to you. She can be pretty persuasive, your mother."

"There's nothing to talk about."

"Tell that to her." Walter sat down on the side of her bed. "You know, honey, I really appreciate that you came home because you thought I needed you to take care of me, but I think you really came home because of your mother."

"That's crazy, Dad. Why would I do that?"

"Because, there are unresolved issues between the two of you that need to be addressed. Until you do that, you will never be able to go forward with your life."

"That's not true."

"Whether it is or not, I'm going downstairs for breakfast. I suggest you get dressed, come downstairs for breakfast and talk to your mother. If nothing else, do it for me."

"All right." Gwen waited for her dad to leave before getting out of bed, hopping in the shower and getting dressed for church. By the time she came downstairs, her dad had already finished breakfast.

"About time," her mother said. "I'll warm up your French toast."

"No thanks, Mom. I'm not hungry."

"Nonsense. You're always hungry for my French toast."

Her dad stood up.

"Where are you going, Dad?"

"I've had my breakfast. I'll leave so you gals can talk."

"Dad, no," Gwen protested but he was already out the door.

"Sit down." Laura put a plate of French toast in front of her and poured her some coffee. "First you eat, then we can talk."

"There's nothing to talk about."

"Eat. Talk later. Or you listen and I'll talk. How would that be?" Laura sat down across from her.

"Pretty much like my whole life." Gwen picked up the fork and started eating.

"I know you're upset with me over that whole thing with Officer Kelley."

"It's not just that. It's this whole year, your Man of the Month club," Gwen started.

Laura raised her hand. "Let me finish."

Gwen put another bite of French toast in her mouth.

"But I only did it out of love."

Gwen rolled her eyes but didn't say anything.

"All right. Maybe it was partially in my self-interest."

"Partially?"

"Look at it from my point of view. I have four children and all of them have moved away. You were my last hope."

Gwen rolled her eyes again.

"Anyway," Laura continued. "Officer Kelley, Liam, he really likes you. And I think you just may like him too. Why punish both of you because of me?"

"I know, Mom. But it's too late. I'll be going back to Chicago in a few weeks. That's not enough time. It's over."

"Okay." Laura sat back and thought for a moment. "How about this? One more man of the month, for June. I'll find someone great. I promise."

"Like all the other ones? Besides, I just told you, it's too late. Too late for me and Liam. Too late for anyone else." Gwen shook her head as she took another bite of French toast.

"What if I tell you, you can have the T-bird if you don't like this guy?"

"I would say you are crazy."

"But you would do it?"

"For the T-bird. Sure. Who wouldn't?"

"You don't even have to stay for the whole date. Five minutes. If you don't like the guy, you're out."

"And I get the T-bird?"

"That's the deal." Laura offered her hand.

"Deal." Gwen shook her mom's hand.

"Good. Now that that's settled, what's this I hear about you leaving seminary?"

"I'm not leaving. I just don't know that I'm cut out to be a pastor. I'm changing majors."

"And then what?"

"Maybe I'll try out for Second City in Chicago."

"Oh no. That won't do at all. I hope I didn't have anything to do with this vocation crisis."

"No, Mom. This one is all on me."

"Because if I did, maybe I can fix it."

"There's no fixing it, Mom. If I'm not called to ordination, better to find out now than ten years from now after I've damaged who knows how many church members with my ineptitude."

"If you say so." Laura shrugged.

"I know so."

"You know, your dad thinks we have unresolved issues between us. Says that's why you came here for your internship." Laura glanced over at Gwen, waiting for her response.

"No more than most mothers and daughters." This time it was Gwen who shrugged.

"I know. That's what I said. So, we're good, right?"

"Well, there is the matter of how you ruined my childhood."

"Like most mothers and daughters, right? That's past. We're good now, right?" Her mother paused, then added. "No need for a mother-daughter heart-to-heart? Because I can do that if that's what you want."

"No, Mom. We're good," Gwen insisted.

"That's a relief. But, you know, if you ever need to talk …"

"Sure, Mom. Now I've got to get to church." Gwen left her mom in the kitchen cleaning up. Seemed appropriate. Was it possible her mom was taking responsibility for her own messes?

Chapter 51

The afternoon sun was still high in the sky despite the hour as Gwen locked the door of the rectory behind her. Daylight savings time. There was no way Sam was getting out. She still didn't understand how he got out that one night, but she took no more chances.

She looked at the church parking lot and was surprised at the number of cars there. Must be a meeting or an activity she didn't know about. This was to be her last gathering with the youth group. She had ordered cake and ice cream. Others were bringing pop, chips, and other snacks. They were going to plan out their activities for the summer. Then some other hapless intern would take over and run the youth group.

When she arrived at the classroom where they had been meeting, no one was there. She heard noise coming from the church hall so she proceeded down the corridor to the hall and saw, not only the members of the youth group, but the young adult group, students from her Bible study, Liz's husband and two children, and even members of her internship committee. There was no surprise shouted as she walked in. Instead there were long faces.

"What's going on?" Gwen asked.

"That's what we're here to ask you." Jacob stepped forward.

"I thought we were going to have the end-of-year party and plan activities for the summer. I guess I thought wrong."

"We heard you were dropping out of the ordination process. When were you going to tell us?" Jacob asked.

"Never?" Gwen attempted a smile. "How did you find out?"

"That would be me." Her mother was in the back of the hall, sheepishly holding up her hand.

"I should have known."

"I only did it because I thought they had a right to know."

"Yes, Vicar Gwen. Were you going to sneak away without telling us?" Josie asked.

"That was the plan. I didn't think it mattered. Apparently, not so good a plan."

"Why?" Grace asked. "What did we do wrong?"

"You didn't do anything wrong. Why would you think that? It was me, all my fault. I'm sorry. I failed you, and now it seems I did it again."

"You didn't fail us," Leon stepped forward. "If it hadn't been for you, I never would have met Lesley here. Or Roger or Gordon. We would still be all alone."

"I don't know what we would have done without you there the last months of my wife's life. She always looked forward to your visits," Liz's husband said.

"But you, Alex." Gwen looked over at Alex. "You would have been better off without me, right?"

"How do you know that? If I hadn't done that particular dumb thing, I probably would have done another," Alex said.

"Only then you wouldn't have been there to help us through it," Jacob added.

Alex's mother came forward, urged by his dad. "And I'm sorry for blaming you for Alex's accident. I guess it was easier to blame you than blame myself. I was so angry and that anger needed a target. You were an easy target."

Then Mrs. Wickersham, the chair of her internship committee stepped forward, pushed by the other members of the committee. "And I apologize for being so critical and unsupportive of you. I see now that was not what the committee was for. We were supposed to help you, not tear you down. We failed you. I'm sorry."

"I appreciate your support now, but what if I'm just not called to ministry," Gwen said.

Adelle came forward from the back of the hall.

"There is more than one way to be called by God. Sometimes God calls us in the quiet of the night, in the depths of our heart, while at prayer. Other times God calls us through God's people. Listen to God's people. They just may be speaking for God."

"I don't know. This is all so confusing."

"You don't have to answer now, but you do need to answer us sometime before you leave. Don't just slip away without telling us," Adelle said.

"So, I can think about it?"

"And pray about it." Adelle looked about the room. "Why all the long faces? This is supposed to be a party. Let's get the party started."

Her mother brought out the cake and ice cream and starting serving pieces. The youth group members brought out the rest of the snacks as people kept coming up to Gwen, thanking her for her service and telling her how much she meant to them. Eventually the crowd thinned out, leaving Gwen alone with the youth group.

"You were a lot more fun than the last intern," Jacob said. "We'll miss you. You will keep in touch, won't you?"

"Of course. You've given me a lot to think about. All of you. I'm going to miss you too." She surprised herself when she realized it was true. She would never forget this youth group or this year.

Chapter 52

"How come you weren't there, at my ambush the other night? You knew about it, didn't you?" Gwen collared Pastor Joe the next day.

"Not much goes on at St. Luke's that I don't know about. I figured this was between you and the congregation. You needed to hear what they had to say without my influence. What did they say?"

"They were upset that I wasn't planning to go on for ordination. Thought they had failed me, that it was their fault."

"One of the realities of being a pastor is that your congregation can feel like they are to blame for things that happen in their pastor's life. Kind of the way kids feel blame for their parents' divorce. I know when I was going through a rough time with my first wife and it looked like we were going to divorce, even though I tried to keep it from the church, they still sensed something was going on."

"I guess it was wrong for me not to tell them before this."

"A beginner's mistake. It's a challenge, knowing how much to share with your congregation and what to keep private. You don't have to share everything. You have a right to a private life, but you can't keep them entirely in the dark. You'll learn over time, if you chose to continue on to ordination and become a pastor."

"If I continue."

"Are you re-considering?"

"Adelle said that sometimes God calls us through other people. She said I needed to listen to what my people were saying."

"A wise woman. Did you finally learn something?"

"Maybe I have."

"Then you don't have to go anymore."

"Ha ha, Pastor. Very funny. You know I've already had my last session with Adelle."

"And it took you all year to learn something." Pastor Joe smiled. "Now, about the ordination question."

"I still don't know. Maybe I'll give it more time before I decide."

"Another wise woman. You don't have to decide today."

Or the next, or the next, Gwen thought. She had all next year to figure it out.

Chapter 53

Another blind date at Giglio's, the downtown Italian restaurant. Her mother had made the arrangements. Gwen did not want to go there. It had been the scene of too many unpleasant dates this past year. She wanted to put all of that behind her.

"This will be different," her mom assured her.

"That's what you always say."

"Just show up. Why do you have to make this so difficult?"

Gwen showed up five minutes early. Her mom was waiting for her.

"What are you doing here?"

"I've arranged for the perfect table. I want this date to go without a hitch."

"Having you here isn't exactly my idea of a perfect date."

"Don't worry. You won't even know I'm here."

Gwen doubted that. She sat down at the table in the corner by the fireplace, her back to the door.

"He's here. Don't turn around," her mom whispered.

"Mom, get out of here." Gwen turned around and saw Liam approaching the table with a large bouquet of calla lilies.

"Your mom said you like them." He held out the bouquet. "Or was that a mistake too. Listening to your mom, I mean."

"No, they're lovely." Gwen took the bouquet then looked for a place to put them on the small table.

"Before you say anything else, would you just listen?" He sat down next to her and reached for her hand. "Gwendolyn Thompson, would you do me the great honor to allow me to be your man of the month for this month and the next and the next?"

Gwen looked at her slender hand, thinking how well it fit into his larger one. "Let's take it one month at a time," she said. "You know I'm going back to Chicago next week. And if I'm ordained, I don't know where the church will send me, but it won't be Cascade Falls."

"I never said I was married to Cascade Falls. I'm sure there will be a police department wherever you end up. We can work it out. One month at a time."

Gwen smiled. "You know, I both hoped it would be you, and hoped it wouldn't be."

"Why?"

"Because now I won't get the Thunderbird." Gwen smiled at the look on Liam's face. "I'll explain later." She looked about the restaurant and saw her mom and her friends standing by the maître d's stand. "We seem to have an audience."

"You didn't answer my question. May I be your Man of the Month?"

"Yes, you may."

"She said yes," he yelled across the room.

"Kiss her," her mom yelled back.

Liam reached over and gave her a long, slow kiss.

"Good enough for you, Mom?" Gwen yelled at her mother.

"Yes!" Laura gave each of her friends a high five. "I win!"

"You don't really want to stay here, do you?" Liam asked.

"No, do you?"

"Let's get out of here. Where to?"

"Burger Barn," they said in unison. Gwen picked up her flowers and accompanied Liam out of the restaurant as her mother and her friends cheered.

"I always knew it would work out," Gwen heard her mother's friend Bernice say. "Though whether it will last …" Her mother and other friends hit Bernice with menus.

Gwen laughed. Nothing was going to ruin this night.

Chapter 54

Gwen packed the last suitcase into the trunk of her Ford Fiesta and smiled as she looked back at the manse. Another warm summer day. Was it just a year ago she was unpacking her car and moving in? Didn't seem possible. Time to say goodbye to Pastor Joe.

"Ready to go?" Pastor asked as she knocked on the rim of his door.

"Yes. I wanted to thank you for all you did for me this year."

"Okay, but I don't know what I did."

"You didn't let me quit when I wanted to quit."

"I was just worried about my reputation with the seminary." Pastor Joe winked. "Lose too many interns and you don't get anymore."

"Would you just let me thank you."

"You're welcome."

Gwen gave him a hug. "Who knows. Maybe I will end up at Cascade Falls someday. When you are ready to retire or leave for a new challenge."

"Heaven only knows." Pastor Joe shook his head and smiled.

"That's right. Heaven knows," she said as she left.

She went back to the rectory, put Sam on his leash then took one last look about her before locking the door. Soon another intern would arrive and take up residence here.

All she had left to do was turn in her key. She locked Sam in her car then went back to the church office and handed her key to her mom.

"You're not getting away without a hug." Her mom stepped from behind her desk in order to give Gwen a hug. "I'm going to miss you."

"I'm going to miss you too." Gwen said.

"You really mean that?" Laura pulled back and looked at her.

"No one is more surprised than me." Gwen smiled and started for the door. "Thank you for everything, Mom."

"Don't forget to call. Call me when you get there." Laura followed her out of the building. Gwen stopped as her dad drove up in the Thunderbird.

"Dad, what are you doing here with Mom's T-bird?"

"Couldn't let my little girl leave without saying goodbye."

"But we already said goodbye, last night."

"That was last night, this is now. Someone had to drive over your new car."

"My new car?"

"Didn't you tell her?" Her father looked over at her mom.

"And ruin the surprise?" Her mom smiled as she watched Gwen struggle to understand what was happening.

"Surprise? You mean …"

"Yes, the Thunderbird is yours."

"But you love that car."

"I love you more. Besides, you earned it. You're the one who found your 'Man of the Month.'"

"What can I say?" Gwen stammered.

"How about thank you." Laura hugged her daughter as Walter transferred her luggage from the Fiesta to the Thunderbird.

"Thank you," Gwen responded then hugged her dad. "And you too, Dad."

"I take it you and your mom have worked out your issues." Walter squeezed her tight then let her go.

"What issues?" Laura asked.

"Yeah, Dad. What issues?" Gwen smiled at her mom.

"Never mind. Forget I said anything. Drive carefully. There's a lot of horsepower in that car."

Gwen loaded Sam into the back seat of the Thunderbird then climbed in. "Thanks again for the T-bird, Mom."

Laura patted the side of the car. "Don't forget, you're coming home for Christmas."

"Yes, Mom."

"And Thanksgiving too. Don't forget Thanksgiving."

"Love you," Gwen shouted as she rode down the street, leaving her parents standing together in front of the church.

Walter wrapped his arm around Laura as she waved until Gwen was out of sight.

"Are you sure you're okay? I mean, you just gave up your Thunderbird. Gwen is moving back to Chicago and will be moving away from Cascade Falls after ordination. You didn't get what you wanted."

"Who says? My daughter is happy. That's all that matters. Besides, I have other plans ..."

"Now what are you plotting?"

"Nothing. Though I was thinking, a Mustang would be nice." Walter sighed and squeezed his wife as she continued to stare down the street after their daughter.

Gwen pulled up to Liam's house and honked her horn. He was riding with her to Chicago, helping her get settled, then driving back with Sam. He was taking care of Sam while she was at seminary.

"How did you get the Thunderbird?" Liam asked as he climbed in.

"You forget, I won the Man of the Month."

"That you did." He leaned over and kissed her.

"Make sure you take good care of Sam and the T-bird while I'm gone."

"Sam, you, and the Thunderbird too. It doesn't get any better than this."

"No, it doesn't," Gwen smiled as she pulled out of her driveway and squealed down the road. Let the adventure begin!

Note to the Reader:

This is my first, and most likely only attempt at romantic comedy. My mind tends to be of a more serious, melancholy nature. And so, writing comedy was a stretch, but one I enjoyed. I owe a debt of gratitude to Steven Kaplan and his book, *The Comic Hero's Journey,* for his help writing this book.

With my other books, I was careful to stay close to reality. In this book, using Kaplan's guidelines I took an improbable scenario — that of a mother starting a "Man of the Month Club" to find her daughter a husband — added in flawed characters and saw what happened.

Gwen is a flawed, fallible, young woman full of insecurities. One minute she will rush into a situation without thought of danger (as in book five of this series, *Delicious Secrets*, where she and her friend Marcie take on a trafficking gang), and the other she is afraid to commit, afraid of making a mistake. She seeks the security of universal truths she finds in the Lutheran Church, wanting a black and white world with easy answers which is impossible. She wants a relationship, yet is afraid at the same time.

An unlikely person to be a minister, yet God often choses unlikely individuals to be his "heroes" in this world. Individuals who have it all together are likely to get in the way, asserting their own will rather than allowing God to work through them. Gwen is aware of her failings, goes into situations having no clue what to do, yet somehow God works through her.

I'm also indebted to Mickey Haddick, who introduced me to Kaplan and loaned me his copy of his book, and to my friend Lori Tate who gave me the name and inspiration for the Man of the Month Club from her own experiences in the dating scene. The ideas for the crazy first dates came from a web search of terrible dates. You can't make this stuff up!

Thank you for suspending belief, accepting this premise and joining me on this journey. I hope you have as much fun reading it as I did writing it. If you enjoyed this book, please leave a review on Amazon, Goodreads and any other outlets. Your comments would be appreciated and mean so much to me in terms of helping others notice my book. You, the reader, have the power to make or break a book in this day of e-marketing and social media.

Thank you again for reading *Man of the Month*. Stay tuned for the next book in the series, *Rebound*!

Patricia M. Robertson

Other Novels by Patricia M. Robertson

Dreamweavers – Dream again, wherever you are in your life.

Buying Time – Visit the peace movement during the Cold War era of Ronald Regan, SDI (Strategic Defense Initiative) and MAD (Mutually Assured Destruction).

Land of Deep Waters - Honduras, land of deep waters, a country torn apart by civil unrest, violence and poverty: Is it possible to go back?

Magnificent Failure - Is it possible to start over? Failures in the eyes of the world and their own eyes, Diane and Jake found each other.

Dancing Through Life Series

Dancing on a High Wire – What do you do when life knocks you off balance? Join Sara, Joy and Esther as each seeks to find a "new normal" and regain their balance on this high wire we call life.

Still Dancing - Some phone calls we love, others we hate, like the ones Pastor Joe receives from his daughter's school. Or the one Dale received at work, letting him know his wife, Joy, had fallen and was in route to the hospital by ambulance. Could her cancer be back?

A Slow Waltz - The road to healing from loss is a slow one, sometimes going backward and sideways before going forward. Sometimes the biggest barrier to healing lies within us. Join Dale, Kathleen, Ava and others as they journey to forgiveness and healing.

An Irish Slip Step -The Irish slip jig is set in 9/8 signature time, unusual and a little off balance, like life! Kathleen didn't know about the slip jig, but she knew about slipping up. As did Chloe's, whose life was knocked off balance by an unplanned pregnancy. And then there was that fiery red-head, Mary Helen, who fell in love with an

American soldier. Was it a slip-step or one of life's fortuitous missteps that brought them precisely where they were meant to be?

Delicious Secrets - Pastor Joe's church secretary retired a year ago. Since then he has struggled to find the right person to fill this position. Enter Marcie, a twenty-something college dropout, trying to find her way in the world. A church secretary was the last job she would have chosen, but she makes the best of it by entertaining herself with real and imagined secrets about church members, until she stumbles upon a secret she would rather not know. Once known, there was no turning back.

Beautiful Questions - Some questions are so big, they can take a lifetime to answer. They are big enough for you to live in, walk around in them, taste them, touch them, and test them. They are beautiful questions. What are the beautiful questions in your life? Join Gwen and others as they ask beautiful questions.

Lyrical Dance - What do you do when all you've ever known about yourself, what gave your life meaning, is wiped away? How do you get it back?

Freedom Dance - All of her life, Letty has struggled to fit in. There is the middle-class world of her parents, the white middle-class world of her friends, and the poverty-stricken world of her cousins. Will she ever find her place in the world?

About the Author

Patricia M. Robertson is an author, speaker and spiritual director, who is committed to helping individuals find God in their every day experience. She also is author of a companion non-fiction book to *Still Dancing, Walking with Families through the Dying Process*, as well as *Walking with Families through Grief,* a companion to *A Slow Waltz*.

She has written other non-fiction books and writes a weekly blog and monthly newsletter. She has a Doctor of Ministry and over thirty-five years of experience in ministry to families. She currently is enjoying her own love story with her husband, Jack, grown children and grandchildren. For more information about her ministry, go to www.patriciamrobertson.com.

REBOUND

Jacob was the rebound king, both on the court and off. He got up after being knocked down as if nothing had happened. He picked up and dropped women as quickly as the ball in a basketball game. Life's hurts and challenges slid off his shoulders. Until he met the one woman who was impervious to his charms. Had he finally found a love to last a lifetime, only to lose her?

Josie was determined to not let anything, including CMT, a disabling nerve disorder, keep her from reaching her goals, especially not her best friend's attractive brother.

What happens when an irresistible force meets an immovable object? Find out in *Rebound,* book ten of the Dancing through Life Series.